CHOOSE

YOUR

DOOM

This is a work of fiction.
Similarities to persons, living or dead,
are neither intended
nor should be inferred.

ISBN: 978-1-951522-06-3

CHOOSE YOUR DOOM

JOHN URBANCIK

Page 1

You must make a decision. It may seem insignificant, but it will impact the rest of your life—or maybe lead to the end of it, should you choose poorly. It's innocuous enough, but any number of variables may come into play.

First, the facts of the situation: it's a massive house, a Gothic mansion, on a rainy and thunderous night. There's always the option of avoiding the house altogether, but you didn't come alone. You know—your heart knows, if not your head—that your companion, your partner in this venture, your best friend and lover, must be inside that structure. So despite the sharply angled gables, despite the overflowing rain gutters, despite the sounds of wolf song in the distance, you feel compelled. The car is dead, either the battery or the fuel or some plug or belt, something you can't figure out in this deluge. Your cellphone is dead, drained of energy, a darkened brick, a chunk of useless plastic.

Nothing about the house is inviting. Your partner would not simply wander up those steps and willingly enter the house. You would not have. But now, really, do you have the choice to not enter?

You do. But you know the consequences if you don't.

The options are clear. You can walk up to the front door, lift that heavy knocker and, announce yourself. Go to Page 2.

You can sneak around the back, climb in through a window, perhaps conduct a search without alerting the house's residents to your presence. Go to Page 3.

You can enter through the cellar doors in the back. Though that seems foolhardy, there's a lock in place but it's open, so you don't have to break in. Go to Page 4.

You can abandon your partner, friend, and lover, and leave the car and the house. Go to Page 5.

You can wait, sitting in the front seat of your dead car as the rain pummels its roof. If so, go to Page 6.

You walk straight up to the front door, climb the rain-slick steps of the porch, lift the lion's head knocker, and knock.

The door swings open as you knock. It was not latched.

Still, you knock, three times, the sound echoing through the darkness with a volume that competes with the thunder. No one answers.

Peering inside, the foyer is three stories tall, with one long window above the door letting in only the light of the storm, and a thin chandelier.

The coat rack is empty. The table beside the front door is caked with dust, but a candelabra with three lit pillars provide most the light for the room. Stairs ascend into darkness. Another doorway goes deeper into the house. There's a room to the side, an office of some sort, perhaps a den.

You pick up the candelabra to provide you with light as you search for your lover.

Ascend the stairs. Go to Page 30.

To enter the office, go to Page 142.

To pass through the doorway, go to Page 233.

Around the back of the house, the darkness is deeper and the storm more torrential, yet one of the dozen windows is open, if only a crack. You're able to push it up all the way and climb into an enormous kitchen. You clamor through the empty sink into a room filled with stainless steel and skillets hanging from racks over a gigantic stovetop. Shelves, hold pots and pans of every size. The walk-in freezer is closed, but there's a wet spot — perhaps melted ice? — visible along the edge of the door.

There are two ways out of the kitchen: into the dining room, or into a long hall. Neither is very well lit, but there's enough to maneuver through either. The hallway looks empty, and obviously leads somewhere, and it sounds like there may be someone eating in the dining room.

To enter the dining room instead, go to Page 68.

If you prefer to try the hall, go to Page 82.

If you would like to go into the walk-in freezer, go to Page 109.

The cellar door leans at an angle against the side of the house. The padlock is undone, and the sounds of the thunderstorm mask any noise made by pulling one of the doors open. It bangs down, but you doubt it's revealed your presence to anyone or anything.

The steps are rough concrete, short and steep, and bring you below the house into a dark cellar awash with shadows. There's halls, there's a pile of lawn equipment—hoes and rakes and the like—leaning against a wall, and there's shelves filled with old paint cans, wooden boxes of varying sizes, and blackened, moldy books that have seen better days.

Rainwater leaks into the basement in several places you can see right at the start, but their sounds mingle with the storm raging outside.

There's a flashlight. Turning it on rewards you with a weak, dingy beam of light cuts through the gloom.

Straight ahead, there's more shelves and more darkness. Go to Page 40.

From here, you can go left, from where you hear the softest possible strains of music which may or may not be music at all. Go to Page 65.

You can go to the right, which seems utterly silent. Go to Page 83.

Obviously, this is a game you cannot play. You must not play. Someone or something wicked is attempting to do something most especially nasty, and you will have no part of it. Your partner is either beyond saving, has managed to save themselves, or is a part of the entire effort in the first place.

So you abandon your car, you abandon your lover, you abandon the spooky house on this rainy, thunderous night, and you walk up the road in the direction you were headed. The town is not so far away. You will find a working telephone, or a mechanic with a tow truck to rescue your car, or a police officer with a gun and a badge and a fair bit of bravery.

The rain soaks you thoroughly and shows no sign of abating. The thunder matches the rhythm of your steps. Despite the relentless noise, eventually you hear something moving in the woods—not because the thing stalking you is careless, but because it has decided to reveal itself. Ahead of you, red eyes nearly glow in the gloom as the loping thing rises to its full height. Its claws hang at its sides, its hands open, its teeth strobing in the staccato lightning.

If you choose to stand and face the creature, go to Page 11.

You can run back toward the house, go to Page 54.

Or go through the woods to try getting around the creature. Go to Page 251.

Waiting may not seem like an act of bravery, but it's definitely the most sensible option. Surely, your partner merely wandered away to relieve themselves behind a tree, rather than enter that big spooky house at the top of the hill.

The sound of rain on the car's roof, however, is hypnotic, and the only thing you hear. There's no radio, no phone, no other sound except your own even breathing. The rhythm is calming, even, and maybe you drift toward sleep. You don't dream, merely doze, merely slip through consciousness, through a series of whatever thoughts occupy your calm little mind.

Time slips, you don't know how much of it, until you gradually become aware something is wrong, something amiss, something not quite right. You're not sure what it is. Your partner hasn't returned, there's been no movement at the house—has there?—or from the woods on either side of the road, and no sign of any other cars, not even a raging semi blasting through the night.

No, it's the color of the rain. Red. Like blood. Like cherry Flavor Aid. Like the memories of nightmares undreamt since you were but a child.

Do you continue to wait in the car? Go to Page 31.

Do you brave the red rain and investigate? Go to Page 38.

You take a breath and sit and ask for deeper explanations, as though I can give you anything that will satisfy your insatiable hunger. I like the idea, though, so I'll tell you this: it started long ago, in a time already romanticized by today's youth, then unborn, when I first held a pen and first changed a fate. It was inspiring, yes, but also terrifying, and in those earliest stories I tried to steer my own fate. Maybe sometimes I succeeded, but maybe sometimes I only wrote silly and saccharine poetry that failed to impress.

I like you, I'll tell you that for free. I don't do this because I wish you harm or horror. I don't do this because of anything you deserve. I'm not the arm of Karma delivering justice or vengeance or balance. I am merely the storyteller, not unlike one of the old gods, a creature like you, armed with a pen and an imagination that keeps me awake under the light of the moon.

And because I like you, I'll let it end, here and now, without bloodshed. You've survived, the story is over, and there are no more choices to make. But I hope it was worth it, cheating like this, skipping around as though this were some simple linear tale from Point A to Point B. It was never that, and never intended to be that, and you've apparently done something wrong because now you'll never be able to rescue you're lover. I hope you're satisfied.

Your story is done.

You stand before the judge and say, "Not guilty, your honor. Not guilty at all. I didn't do this, I didn't have anything to do with this. I want justice, and that cannot be had if the police don't really look into it."

"Oh, the police have looked," says the cop, but the judge bangs his gavel.

"I'll have order," the judge says. The courtroom settles down somewhat reluctantly. They think you're guilty. They don't *think* it; they know it. They know it, but it's not true, not even remotely true.

"Have you any evidence," the judge asks, "any whatsoever, that might prove your innocence?"

If you have no evidence, go to Page 14.

If you have evidence, go to Page 47.

It's a small church—no, it's a small cathedral, set in a depression in the hillside so it doesn't look quite as tall as it is. There are spires, gargoyles on the walls, and towers, and the thunder resounds within the church bells.

The front doors are massive, twice as tall as you and then some, saints and bishops carved into the wall above it. The door is ajar, and you slip easily inside. It's dark, but not completely—there are lights on some of the columns, and candles on the altar and at prayer stations to either side. There's a font of holy water immediately beyond the doors, and three rows of pews leading to the front.

Organ pipes flank the altar, and there's a massive statue of—presumably Jesus, but the head's been knocked off and is missing. The break looks fresh and sharp, though there's no sign of the head on the ground.

After that, you notice other things awry: panes missing from the stained glass windows, cracks in others, tapestries that have been shredded and hang now like dripping blood.

The sanctuary around the altar includes those pipes, several statues turned to face away from the altar—except the headless one—and a crypt where a bishop or cardinal of some sort has been interred. Between you and the sanctuary, there's a nave reaching to impossible heights—higher than seems possible considering the size outside. The shadows contribute to the sensation of infinity. On either side as you approach the altar, there's a seating area for the choir. And on the left, there are a series of alcoves and doorways.

Additionally, there's one person kneeling in the pews, facing the altar, their back to you. It could be anyone. It could be your lover.

Go to the doors and alcoves on the side of the cathedral. Go to Page 266.

Leave the cathedral Go to Page 284.

Approach the person. Go to Page 318.

You climb back in and pull shut the door. The red rain falls more and more heavily, and it doesn't take long to realize the red droplets are dinging the hood of your car, cracking the glass of the windshield, making craters in the roof.

There's no place to hide from the rain. Spider web cracks spread across all the windows and mirrors. The roof collapses gradually. It's all quite fast, now, as though the rain is a fist and the car merely an old piece of origami to be crushed and discarded.

Finally, the first piece of crimson hail breaks the window and crashes into dashboard. It sits there like a ruby, gleaming, confident, nearly sentient, challenging you to do something.

Half a second later, perhaps less, an armada of blood hail shatters the windows and rips through the roof and pelts you, embeds itself in your skin, works into your veins. They crack your bones and shatter your skull and spill your blood and steal your life.

You chose poorly.

You have no weapons, but you know there's no point in running. You may have no weapons, but you also know you're not the kind of athlete who could easily escape an apex predator such as this.

It's a massive thing, rising in the darkness, a wolfish creature growling at the back of its throat. It steps forward, a single intimidating movement, slow and deliberate, giving you every chance to run.

You may tremble, but you stand your ground.

Another step, and it's closed the gap between you unnervingly quick. Its fur is matted by the rain. You see yourself reflected in its eyes. Another step closer, however, and you realize the truth of the creature.

It's human. It's tall and muscular, but it's at least mostly human, or it was once before as human as you. It draws in a great breath through massive flaring nostrils. It looks down at you, licks its lips, and speaks in a guttural, rough, deep voice. "You wouldn't make much of a meal, would you?"

If you agree, go to Page 49.
If you disagree, go to Page 56.

Descending the steps, she knocks three times. "I'm so pleased to have found you," she says as the door swings open.

Inside, it's a typical basement room, with bland off-white walls and a circle of maybe twenty folding chairs, mostly occupied by people wearing robes. Your guide has taken the last robe from the pegs along the outer wall and entered the circle so smoothly, you're no longer sure where she's gone.

"Welcome," the leader of the congregation says. "You are the stranger, as foretold, who will wake the sleeping god. Please." He gestures toward an empty chair in the center of the circle. "Sit."

"I don't know what you're talking about," you tell him.

He shakes his head and smiles. "Doesn't matter. All we need is your blood."

Stealthily, congregants have already circled around you, so even if you want to flee there's no place to go. They've got you by the arms, two on either side. They propel you forward, toward the chair, which has been placed atop a black mirror reflecting only the pale recessed lights in the ceiling.

They do their best to not step on the mirror as they force you into the chair. You're surprised the mirror doesn't crack under your weight.

"The old gods have been sleeping and dreaming and planning and scheming," the leader says, "and awaiting the blood of the stranger who is not merely a stranger but their final descendant."

Apparently, it doesn't matter if you have brothers, sisters, cousins, or children. They've made up their mind.

"This," the leader says, "won't require much."

If you want to relax and trust fate, go to Page 78.

Do you prefer to struggle and try to escape? If so, go to Page 91.

You don't really have that choice. You close your eyes, but you'll open them again later anyhow.

Go to Page 203.

"I don't need to prove I'm innocent," you say. "That's not how it works."

"That," the judge says, "is how it works here." There's laughter in the courthouse, but the judge bangs his gavel. You look to your attorney, who merely shrugs.

"Seeing no other evidence before the court," the judge says, "you shall be held until such time as we are able to clear the court's docket and try you, convict you, and punish you, in full accordance with the law." The judge bangs his gavel. "Officer, please escort our prisoner to his holding cell."

If you will go quietly to your cell, go to Page 20.

To attempt to escape, go to Page 316.

Once you're in the door, your mysterious benefactor slams it shut just as a crack of thunder booms overhead. He motions you to a peephole so you can watch the congregants run past the door as though it wasn't even there.

"I knew they'd be after you, soon as I saw you out there on the street. Are you mad, or what?" he says. He doesn't wait for an answer. "Welcome to the asylum."

Taking in the room, you see it's probably no different than the congregant's place of worship, but here there are a number of people huddled beneath blankets or staring blankly at the walls. It's not a medical facility, and not all of its residents appear to be in need of such an institution, but there are enough of them to make you wonder.

Your benefactor wears a doctor's white lab coat and a stethoscope and spectacles that somehow shrink his eyes. He hasn't shaven recently, but it's not quite a beard scratching through the flesh of his skin.

"Most visitors, as you can see," he says, "become targets of the congregation."

"I appreciate the help," you say.

"Well, you're free to stay as long as you wish."

If you've already stayed as long as you wish, go to Page 93.

If you wish to stay a little longer and let the congregants disperse, go to Page 212.

A narrow alley cuts between two of the buildings. A figure leans against one of those brick walls and, for a moment, watches you approach. As you get closer, the figure nods, turns, and walks deeper into the alley. She pauses briefly to be sure you follow.

You step into the shadows. The figure hasn't gone far. She's stopped halfway down the alley and turned to face you. She smiles. Her features are vague in the dark, but she looks you up and down and says, "You're a stranger."

"I am."

"Walking in the rain."

You admit to that, too.

"Some would say that's a strange thing for a stranger to do."

"My car died," you explain. You would go further, but she stops you.

"I wouldn't say any such thing. The prophecy said you would arrive in a night without moonlight." She lifts her hands and looks toward the sky and the clouds. "I see no moon tonight, stranger."

"Neither do I. But I need..."

She shakes her head ."I can't help you. But I can bring you to the congregation."

"Congregation?"

"I'll explain as we go. Confirmation of your arrival has already spread. They'll all be there by now. All but me."

She wears her hair like Veronica Lake and hides her face under the brim of a hat which at least protects her makeup from the rain. She's got red lipstick, you see that clearly, but all other colors fade to nothing in the murk. She walks behind the buildings that line the edge of town. There's no second street, no further buildings, no sound but the rain and the thunder and the woman's feet tapping out a staccato on the pavement.

"The congregation formed two hundred years ago when the town was founded," she says.

"I have to help..."

She shakes her head. "Either listen to me, or don't, but don't interrupt." When you offer no immediate response, she continues. "The congregation gathers because of the prophecy. Under the shadows on a moonless night, the prophecy promises salvation in the form of a stranger who has lost something valuable."

"My partner," you say.

She shakes her head. "The prophecy isn't that specific. It says, instead, you will usher home the old gods."

Here, you stop. That's enough nonsense. You want help, not a crazy person. But your guide has also stopped, and turned toward a door three steps deep, a green door with flaked paint and rusted hinges.

"We're here," she says.

Follow her inside. Go to Page 12.

To turn back, go to Page 53.

You give the creature a respectable thirty seconds, or what seems like thirty seconds, to disappear into the woods. You stand in the middle of the road in the middle of the rain, surrounded by thunder and lightning bolts, and finally, with the loudest crash of thunder, take off at full speed toward the town that must wait ahead of you.

You don't get five steps before the creature takes you down.

It leaps on you from above, from the treetops, from the storm itself like a rain of teeth and claws. The creature doesn't leave much by which to identify you.

You chose poorly.

The old man watches you approach. He leans back quite comfortable despite the rain. He appraises you thoroughly before saying, "Who are you?"

So you tell him your name, and you tell him your story, about how your car mysteriously died near the spooky house and your partner vanished without a trace.

"And you left them alone?" the old man asks, shaking his head. "Ain't never heard of something so cowardly before. What do you expect, coming into town? To form a posse and rescue your love? Or do you just want to find a warm bed, or perhaps a bellyful of beer? Tell me, child. What do you want?"

If you want to form a posse, go to Page 51.

If you want a warm bed, go to Page 85.

If you want a bellyful of beer, go to Page 102.

If you think this is a rhetorical question that requires no answer, go to Page 262.

The officer escorts you to your cell, the same cell, mumbling the whole time about dirtying his jail with so filthy a murderer. It's obvious no further inquiries will be made, the real killer will go free, and you may never get a chance to avenge your lost lover.

The officer locks you in the cell and says, "I'll be back to feed you."

But the officer never returns.

The day ends, night arrives, and a comet streaks across the sky so brightly you see it even through a barred window about the size of a loaf of bread. It lights up the sky for five minutes, at least, and that's it. That's the last thing you see.

Dawn comes the next morning, dusk comes the next night, but there are no visitors, there's nothing else visible outside that jail cell window. It's just the trees pressed up against the edge of town.

After a few days, you're thirsty, and you're hungry, and you're lonely. The only sounds are the echoes of your own thoughts within your head. Another day arrives and finds you laying on your side on the plank that serves as a bed. You're sore, and surely you're hallucinating, because that's when the aliens enter the jailhouse. Three of them, tall and thin, thinner than models and thinner than heroin addicts, and taller than basketball players, taller than giants. They bend when they enter the jailhouse. They stare at you through the bars and they talk with each other but the language sounds like whistles and clicks. Finally, they come to some sort of agreement and turn to leave.

If you're willing to let these hallucinatory aliens just leave, go to Page 94.

If you want to try to stop them, go to Page 105.

The key is cold when you touch it. You do your best not to actually touch the table, lest its rot rub off on you. But the key and the music box seem unharmed. You wind it two, three times around, and set the music box back on the table. It sings again, and its hauntingly familiar melody reaches through your ears and through pores of your skin, infiltrating your brain and your heart and maybe your soul.

It's familiar, but unamenable, a waltz or something like it, a song so old it predates even the house. When it finishes, you retrieve the key again—you have no choice, you're compelled by something in your veins. You wind the box and set it playing again, and the notes play against your bones.

If you wish to keep playing with the music box and see what happens, go to Page 59.

If you want to try to resist, go to Page 137.

You walk.

The rain accompanies you, and possibly the creature matches your pace unseen in the woods. It's only another ten or twenty minutes before you reach the edge of the town.

It's not much of a town. It's a single street, the road you're already on, and a collection of maybe a dozen structures, mostly two or three stories tall, with anonymous storefronts at street level and dark windows above. There's no stoplight, no streetlamp, and at first nothing to indicate anyone lives here at all except a few cars parked haphazardly along the curb.

In the shadows, the flickering storm highlights and accents faces in the windows, figures in the alleys, and a man sitting on a rocking chair on his porch, as wet by the rain as you.

If you want to approach one of the figures in the shadows, go to Page 16.

If you prefer to approach the man on the rocking chair, go to Page 19.

Looking into the mirror, you meet the valet's eyes, and you attempt to say something—something like hello, a greeting of any sort—but you find the eyes mesmerizing, and the surface of the mirror entrancing.

The valet smiles. Those are cobra eyes and a genie's grin.

"That's right," the valet says, his voice deep and resonant, "step into the mirror."

The voice is compelling. You may try to resist, but already your legs are taking you forward. When you step through the mirror, it's like moving through a waterfall, and you find yourself on the other side—in another big spooky house on another hill, in another anteroom, where the valet wears black instead of white and carries a machete.

Retreat, back through the mirror. Go to Page 52.

Stand and fight. Go to Page 115.

Run past the valet and down the hidden staircase. Go to Page 166.

"On my way into town," you tell the old man, "there was a creature."

"The Wolf," the old man says, nodding. "Yes, we know it well." He gestures to one of the townsfolk. "Show him, Carl."

Carl presents his shotgun. "Silver shot," he says. "We know our woods, and our wolves know us."

Onward you march, a veritable army, up the street, back toward your car and Old Coop's house and your lost lover. The mob makes no sound except for boots on the pavement, which competes with the thunder. You and the old man lead the way. Everyone else is armed, but as you get further from town, you realize the mob is shrinking. Behind you, one by one, your rescue party has been disappearing. You say something about this to the old man.

"It's to do with age," the old man says.

"I don't understand."

"The older you are, the further from town you can walk."

"That...makes no sense."

"Oh, it does," the old man says.

"Some of those people were younger than me."

"You're a stranger," the old man says by way of explanation.

You reach a point where you can see the house again. It stands stark against the black night, silhouetted frequently by the strobe-like lightning. Only the old man has accompanied you this far.

"Okay, that's it for me," the old man says, stopping. "I can go no further."

"Sure you can."

"Go on," the old man says. "Rescue your lover. We'll be waiting for you."

The old man takes one more step, just to show you what he's said is true. He shimmers out of reality and vanishes through the shadows, leaving you alone in the shadow of the house—and of a church hidden in the woods and only visible when you approach from this direction.

It's of the same kind of structure and material as the house, and looks no less promising. But it seems a more likely destination for your partner than a dark house in the middle of nowhere—admittedly, the church is also dark and in the middle of nowhere, but that's semantics.

You can return to the house, walk up to the front door and announce yourself. Go to Page 2.

You can sneak around the back of the house and climb in through a window. Go to Page 3.

You can enter the house through the cellar doors in the back. Go to Page 4.

You can explore the church. Go to Page 9.

You can wait in the front seat of your dead car as the red rain pummels its roof. Go to Page 10.

You know there's nothing behind you that's going to help, and the contradictory whispers won't help you, so you go forward, straight into a room of thick, absolute darkness that swallows the lights of the candles before they can reach your eyes.

From outside, the sounds of the storm disappear entirely. There are no windows—or at least, no windows allowing any light into the room. You can see so little, it's a question of whether the room itself has swallowed all light or if your eyes have failed. Looking back, you see nothing of the room you left or the boy or the storm that had been flashing in the windows just a moment ago. You can't even see the door.

Stepping back, you cannot find the door.

All you see is darkness and all you hear in the silence are the whispers. You reach for one of the candles on your candelabra. You feel the small heat of its flame. You pluck the candle and drop it on the ground.

You don't hear it land.

The whispers grow both more frantic and more distant. They're vanishing.

You bend to retrieve the candle but cannot find it, cannot find anything, not even the floor—though clearly you're kneeling on something. Tentatively, you step forward. You find something to stand on in the darkness.

That's how you spend the rest of your days—how many days, you can't even guess—wandering in the darkness, in complete silence once the whispers fade, not even able to hear your footsteps or your heartbeat. You're not sure you're alive. You imagine things in the darkness, but they're things made of darkness. They're things made of silence.

You chose poorly.

I don't know how you found me. And I don't know what you expect to happen. Here I sit, old fashioned fountain pen in hand—look at how narrow that nib is, almost like a weapon, don't you think?—and yes, it's true, I'm the author of all your troubles this night, but it's not like I have a choice. That's not ink on those pages, that's blood, my blood, and I pour everything I am into the words and into the stories and yes, you have no choice but to follow, but I suppose there's always an option, so I'll give you this one:

If you wish to walk away, go to Page 7.

If you wish to stop me, which I do not advise, go to Page 34.

You say nothing about the creature, confident in your numbers, certain the creature wouldn't attack such a mob.

And that's what you are: a mob. The storm is clearing, so you feel suddenly invigorated, strong, even brave, and that's when you see movement in the woods.

Not on one side. On both. In the treetops above.

Without any other warning, the creatures attack. They come from the right and the left, they come from above, they come in numbers you hadn't even imagined, a dozen of them or more, and they carve their way bloodily through your rescue party.

The creature you met in the street earlier lifts you by your throat, allows you to watch the slaughter of the townsfolk and the feast that follows, and says, "Thank you for the meal, lost little thing."

Then it consumes you.

You chose poorly.

You give the barkeep money and climb out of the bar. You feel as though you've escaped something, though you're not quite sure what. You return to the storm, the relentless rain and the thunder and the wet, and the figures in the shadows.

To approach the figures in the shadows, go to Page 16.

If you want to find the local police station, go to Page 71.

If you want to return to the house, go to Page 74.

The stairs are mercifully silent as you climb. The stairs curve to the right. The landing looks down on the chandelier — long and thin iron and glass, inside of which, in a flash of lightning, you almost see the shadow of a woman staring back at you.

But there's no one and nothing there.

Really.

It's just a chandelier. The ironwork doesn't form the shape of a noose on the inside. That's purely your imagination. A function of the inconsistent shadows.

You cannot examine it more closely under any circumstance. The landing is too far away, and the light of the candelabra is too dim. Instead, you enter a hall and have a choice of a room to the right or the left. Both doors are closed. Or you can continue down the hall, where there's another door to the right.

To enter the first door on the right, go to Page 265.

To enter the second door on the right, go to Page 304.

To enter the door on the left, go to Page 314.

The rain falls more and more heavily with time. You're aware of it now, every passing second, as though a clock ticks inside your head. The seconds pop faster as the rain intensifies. The red droplets are dinging the hood of your car, cracking the glass of the windshield, making little dimples in the roof.

There's no place to hide from the rain. Spider web cracks spread across all the windows and mirrors. The roof collapses gradually. It's all quite fast, now, as though the rain is a fist and the car merely an old piece of origami to be crushed and discarded.

Finally, the first piece of crimson hail breaks the window and crashes into dashboard. It sits there like a ruby, gleaming, confident, nearly sentient, challenging you to do something.

Half a second later, perhaps less, an armada of blood hail shatters the windows and rips through the roof to pelt you, embed itself in your skin, work into your veins. They crack your bones and shatter your skull and spill your blood and steal your life.

You chose poorly.

You rush forward. But you're unarmed, and the bartender is quick with the shotgun. A single shot is enough to make mince of your guts. A second shot does the same to your head.

You chose poorly.

You tell the bartender exactly what you want, and he complies immediately, preparing and serving the drink like an expert. "You know," he tells you, "the dance doesn't start for another hour. But the guest of honor—well, would you like to meet her?"

Yes. Go to Page 112.

No. Go to Page 125.

You bristle at the idea of your fate and destiny in my hands, don't you? I can see it in your eyes. Fine, be that way. I'm in charge here, and so you've come to the end of the story. That's your punishment for skipping around like you have. You didn't think I wouldn't notice, did you? You expected to somehow subvert my wishes?

You forget, this isn't because I wish it. It's because I'm compelled. There's a force driving me that maybe you can never understand. I don't know if you will. I only know you've reached the end of your journey, and your lover remains trapped forever within this story.

You might try to take my pen, or you might pull a knife or revolver from some hidden pocket I'd not foreshadowed, but you're too late. It's over. It's done. The story is at an end. And what did you learn, by trying to cheat me, eh?

Your story is done.

You pick a lollipop of your favorite color, and it's exactly the flavor you expected.

"Yeah, there ain't much to see," the nurse says, propping herself onto a rather large box and sitting with her feet dangling. "Give 'em a tour, the doctor says. He says it every time. It's like all I do around here. I'm a genuine certified registered nurse, you know. I've got skills."

She's looking at you as though she's suggesting her areas of expertise may go beyond typical methods of healing, so you say, "Maybe I better get going."

She pulls the lollipop from her mouth with a smacking noise. "I don't think so."

"What do you mean, you don't think so?"

"I'm afraid you're sick," she says. "Contagious. Infectious. Whatever we've all got, you've got it now, too, so you ain't going nowhere."

When you make a move for the door, the nurse launches herself at you. She's all breasts and lips and cleaver. You don't even know where she got that. She buries it in your back even as she tackles you. You go down together, and she's swinging the large blade again. The blade finds flesh and quantities of blood.

"It's all for the best," the nurse tells you, grinning wickedly, maniacally. "This way, at least, you can't get anyone else sick but me, and I'm already stricken."

The next cut goes for the neck. You're dead before the next cut.

You chose poorly.

You don't have to wait long. They take you to the hanging tree behind the courthouse, a huge oak where they've been hanging murderers for centuries, since before the country was born. Though you are no murderer, you are hooded and hanged, where you dangle until you finally cease to breathe, and your body is left swaying in the breeze for weeks because no one claims it.

You chose poorly.

You do not, liar.

Go to Page 45.

You step out of the car and into the rain. You look up, seeking the source of the strange red rain. The clouds, so high above, seem tinted, but it's actually the reflection of something you hadn't noticed before. Off to the right, hidden in the dark and by the trees, but vaguely aglow at its highest spire, is a small church. The crimson light emanates from there.

It's of the same kind of structure and material as the house, and looks no less promising. But it seems a more likely destination for your partner than a dark house in the middle of nowhere — admittedly, the church is also dark and in the middle of nowhere, but that's semantics.

You can return to the house, walk up to the front door and announce yourself. Go to Page 2.

You can sneak around the back of the house to climb in through a window. Go to Page 3.

You can enter the house through the cellar doors in the back. Go to Page 4.

You can abandon your partner, friend, and lover, and leave the car, the house, and the church. Go to Page 5.

You can explore the church. Go to Page 9.

You can return to the front seat of your dead car as the red rain pummels its roof. Go to Page 10.

You acknowledge the old man's toast, and maybe even say a word yourself before taking a mouthful of beer. It's very possibly the most delicious beer you've ever had. It quenches your thirst and fortifies your loins. You feel emboldened, and maybe you even consider suggesting a rescue party might not be a bad idea.

But quickly, the room is spinning, and your vision is tunneling, and the barkeeper catches hold of your stein before you drop it. She's shaking her head. "A shame," she says. Weakness overcomes you, but you're not dead. Not merely poisoned.

To close your eyes and simply die, go to Page 13.

To face whatever happens next, go to Page 255.

The hall is lined with shelves carrying various abandoned things: ancient phonographs without needles, lamps with unfortunate designs, piles of framed photos, dishes, boxes of moldering clothes, and a generous blanket of spider webs.

And then there's a door. It's a fine door, in good condition, showing no signs of rot or neglect like the rest of the cellar thus far. It opens, and you enter a room of dignified magnificence. It's a wine cellar, a long room with brick columns and brick walls and an arched ceiling, and electric lights in sconces along the columns.

On one wall, there are displays of particular bottles of wine, five or six at a time, put together in the way you might hang artwork on a wall. The other wall is rows upon rows of wine racks, corks facing out, along with a table and a massive hand-crank wine opener. Ahead, there's another room, without a door, and barrels stacked three high in careful precision.

There's movement in the next room. Perhaps your lover? To investigate, go to Page 287.

To explore the wine cellar more closely first, go to Page 303.

The zombies reach for you and grab at you, and you use your fists and all your martial arts skills. The bartender, when he reaches the hallway, keeps his shotgun trained on you but says, "Looks like you've met some of the guests."

The zombies don't need weapons. The zombies don't feel pain, so none of your blows have any effect. When you try to retreat, the bartender swings the butt end of the shotgun into your face, throwing you back toward the zombies, one of which catches your arm. Its grip is unbreakable. Sure, they move slowly, but they move relentlessly, and they relish fresh meat.

You've become zombie food. The bartender, looking on, shakes his head and continues cleaning glasses. It's a long and ultimately pointless death.

You chose poorly.

You try to evade the question. "My partner is missing out there somewhere," you tell the nurse.

"So...you're committed?"

"Yes."

"I see." The nurse nods, then grins and says, "That's fine. That's good. I understand, I do. I can't help you, I can't go with you, I'm going to hold on to you in my heart forever, but I will do what I can to help. This way."

The nurse leads you out of the storage room and deeper down the hall, to a back door that exits the building in the rear. None of the congregants are in sight. She lowers her voice and confides, "The doctor, he would have killed you, you know that, right?"

You didn't, but you say, "Thanks."

She points in a direction. "That way, you'll go back the way you came, out of town and toward Old Coop's house, where I'm sure you'll find the lover you've lost."

You thank the nurse. She insists on a hug and kisses your cheek and closes the door both quickly and quietly, leaving you on your own to head out of town and back down the road toward your dead car and the old house—and, as you approach, a church, which you hadn't previously seen.

It's of the same kind of structure and material as the house, and looks no less promising. But it seems a more likely destination for your partner than a dark house in the middle of nowhere—admittedly, the church is also dark and in the middle of nowhere, but that's semantics.

You can return to the house, to the front door, to lift that heavy knocker and announce yourself. Go to Page 2.

You can sneak around the back of the house to climb in through a window. Go to Page 3.

You can enter the house through the cellar doors in the back. Go to Page 4.

You can explore the church. If so, go to Page 9.

You can wait in the front seat of your dead car as the red rain pummels its roof. Go to Page 10.

You leave whoever is showering to their privacy and step away.

If you want to continue past them down the hall, to the right, go to Page 274.

If you would rather return to the wine cellar, go to Page 295.

You run into the woods wearing handcuffs, but you can't be sure if you're headed toward the creature you encountered last night or toward the old house, or in some other direction entirely. The sound of pursuit fades behind you, and maybe you'll manage to get away after all.

But after running blindly for too long, you reach a trap. It closes around you, a giant net that snatches you from the ground and dangles you in the air. Almost immediately, a primitive family surrounds you.

"That's sure bigger than a possum," says the little boy.

The father says, "We'll dine well today."

And that's exactly what they do. They run you through a spit and roast you slowly over hot coals until you are good and dead and ready for eating. When they dine, the judge joins them.

You chose poorly.

You swing. You miss. The old man's fast and he evades you easily and breaks out in laughter. "That wasn't half bad," he says, backing down. "Maybe you ain't a coward, after all."

"I just want to find my partner."

The old man nods. He asks, "You need help?"

Go to Page 51.

You bow to the court and present your evidence: the old man's testimony, primarily, a conversation a recent murderer could not have had. "Unless you think me mad," you add.

"That," the judge says, "is circumstantial at best."

"And my car," you say, "stuck on the side of the road, unable to start. I couldn't possibly arrange for that."

"Teenage boys have been making such arrangements for years," the judge says. "You should consider it an honor, that I think you more capable than a typical teenage boy. Have you anything else to support your claim?"

You look to your attorney, who merely shrugs.

"Seeing no other evidence before the court," the judge says, "you shall be held until such time as we are able to clear the court's docket and try you, convict you, and punish you, in full accordance with the law." The judge bangs his gavel. "Officer, please escort our prisoner to his holding cell."

If you will go quietly to your cell, go to Page 20.

To attempt to escape, go to Page 316.

Before she can close her hands arounds you or cast a spell or call down skunk apes by the dozen, you run back the way you came—running not being the easiest thing to do in these murky waters.

One wrong step, and you plunge into an underwater hole. The swampy water grabs you and drags you under. Vines in the muck tug at your legs and arms. You've lost your stick, and you can't break the surface to take a breath. You hear splashing, but it's probably not alligators—it's probably just you.

Your next breath is actually a lungful of swamp, neither tasty nor rich in oxygen. You can't see, but you feel the big alligator's jaws closing on you, and you hear or imagine the swamp witch cackling behind you as you can't decide whether to drown first or be eaten.

Either way, the swamp takes and keeps you, and you never reemerge from its waters.

You chose poorly.

"Can't say that I would," you tell the creature. "Hardly worth the effort at all."

The creature is well within your personal space. It circles around you, scraping one claw across your shoulder and the back of your neck, possibly drawing blood but it's hard to know in the rain. You stand straight, as tall as you're able, but you're at the edge of control. The thunder booms with the creature's every step.

"Hardly any effort at all," the creature says.

You don't answer.

The creature snarls, then dismisses you and walks into the woods.

If you want to take advantage of the creature's absence and run, go to Page 18.

If you want to continue forward at your previous pace, go to Page 22.

You enter the room.

As you do, the chandelier bursts into life, albeit dimly, illuminating the room and sharpening the shadows. The room is only just large enough for a half dozen statues on every wall. It's like a museum, the statues all perfect in form and structure. They're crowded together because they never belonged here. They look extraordinarily lifelike, as though heroes and goddesses of ages past were caught in the midst of battle or bathing or just waking up and stretching their arms to catch the first rays of sunlight.

The shadows give them a sinister tone.

There are crates, too, unopened, scattered about and stacked on each other, some hidden behind the statues, which are not arranged in display but rather for storage.

The panel behind you slides shut. There doesn't appear to be any obvious way back. However, there are two doors, to your right and left.

The right door is ajar. To go through it, go to Page 258.

The left door is closed tight. To go through it, go to Page 266.

"I need help," you admit. "To rescue my true love."

The old man grins. It's a beautiful, wonderful grin. He says, "Then a rescue, we shall mount." He calls to the shadows, to the windows, to the townsfolk. "There's trouble brewing at old Coop's mansion again."

Volunteers emerge from the darkness, first one or two, then ten, finally almost thirty of them, perhaps all the men and women of the town, with pitchforks and torches and grumblings about old Coop's ghost and the murders that took place so many years ago. They're ready and willing and capable, and soon you find yourself and the old man leading an army back toward the old house.

If you want to warn the old man about the creature you met, go to Page 24.

If you don't feel the need, go to Page 28.

The way the mirror version of the valet grins, you know retreat is the wisest option. You step backwards, expecting the waterfall sensation to cover you again, but instead press against cold glass.

From the other side of the mirror, the original valet, all in white, lets loose a Caribbean laugh. On this side, he swings the machete and severs your head in a single, clean stroke.

You chose poorly.

Obviously, you're not going to follow this woman with her crazy talk of congregations and old gods into some basement worship room. You turn and, as it seems appropriate, run. You run back the way you came, alongside the buildings that make up the town, and down the very same alley. A glance behind you reveals two dozen pursuers in hooded cloaks surging through the shadows like living things.

In the alley, a door opens and a man says, "Quick, in here! It's safe!"

You've got time to get in through that door and shut out the alley before the congregation catches up—but only barely.

If you race for the opened door, go to Page 15.

If you ignore the offer, go to Page 57.

You've never heard a wolf laugh before. You're sure of it. It's a sound you'd remember, and a sound you'll remember for the rest of your life—however short it may be. As you run up the street, back toward your car and the old spooky house and your missing partner, the wolf's laughter is louder than the rain and louder than the thunder.

You half expect it to pounce on you as you run, but that doesn't happen. You make it back to the house—and your dead car, still dead—and also a church hidden behind the trees so that you couldn't see it walking the other direction.

It's of the same kind of structure and material as the house, and looks no less promising. But it seems a more likely destination for your partner than a dark house in the middle of nowhere—admittedly, the church is also dark and in the middle of nowhere, but that's semantics.

You can return to the house, walk up to the front door and announce yourself. Go to Page 2.

You can sneak around the back of the house and climb in through a window. Go to Page 3.

You can enter the house through the cellar doors in the back. Go to Page 4.

You can explore the church. Go to Page 9.

You can return to the front seat of your dead car as the red rain pummels its roof. If so, go to Page 10.

"How can I help?" you ask. You don't raise your voice, since sound seems to carry.

She smiles. It's a beautiful smile. "The water's not deep," she says.

And it's not. It's thick and murky, but you grab a stick and use it to test the depth. It's not even so high as your knees. You step carefully into the water. The lakebed sucks at your feet like the path, but doesn't pull you in.

You use the stick to check ahead of you, to make sure you don't accidentally step into a chasm or stumble over knotted roots. The water resists you, and the mud underneath becomes thicker and more difficult to traverse. Despite this, you're halfway to the raft when her eyes grow wide and she says, "Alligator!"

You look back. The alligator—easily ten feet or longer—is slipping into the water behind you, exactly where you stepped in. Its red eyes glow.

If you want to fight the alligator with your stick, go to Page 58.

If you want to abandon caution and run to the raft, go to Page 163.

You're offended by the wolf's offhand dismissal of you. "I'd make an excellent meal," you tell the wolf. "I'm grade A prime meat. You've never tasted anything so good." Which, really, seems like you're asking for it to devour you there and then.

The wolf, however, snarls and steps away but takes a big, deep inhalation. "Have you been dining on wolfsbane? Quicksilver running through your veins?"

You smile. That's all the answer you're capable of giving.

The wolf sneers and retreats into the woods.

If you want to take advantage of the creature's absence and run, go to Page 18.

If you want to continue forward at your previous pace, go to Page 22.

You ignore the door and reach the main street. The thunder growls and the street itself seems to tremble. The congregants emerge from shadows on every side of you. You spin, you twirl, you even put up a fight, but they quickly overpower you.

They drag you back to their place of worship, a typical basement room with bland off-white walls and a circle of maybe twenty folding chairs. Their leader stands near the center of the room. "Welcome," he says. "You are the stranger, as foretold, who will wake the sleeping god. Please." He gestures toward an empty chair in the center of the circle. "Sit."

"I don't know what you're talking about," you tell him.

He shakes his head and smiles. "Doesn't matter. All we need is your blood."

Stealthily, congregants have already circled around you, so even if you want to flee there's no place to go. They've got you by the arms, two on either side. They propel you forward, toward the chair, which has been placed atop a black mirror reflecting only the pale recessed lights in the ceiling.

They do their best to not step on the mirror as they force you into the chair. You're surprised the mirror doesn't crack under your weight.

"The old gods have been sleeping and dreaming and planning and scheming," the leader says, "and awaiting the blood of the stranger who is not merely a stranger but their final descendant."

Apparently, it doesn't matter if you have brothers, sisters, cousins, or children. They've made up their mind.

"This," the leader says, "won't require much."

If you would like to relax and trust fate, go to Page 78.

Do you prefer to struggle and try to escape? If so, go to Page 91.

You turn to face the advancing alligator and jab at it with your stick. You poke its massive jaws. You go for the eyes but miss. It's too big to get fully under the water for the moment, so it's easy to find, and you thrust the stick at it like an epee, repeatedly, until it finally veers silently aside and slides away.

You watch it go before continuing forward.

A few more steps, and you reach the raft. The woman on the raft holds out a hand to help you onto the raft.

Accept her hand and go to Page 80.

Refuse her hand and offer your own, go to Page 87.

It's so easy to keep the music going. The key, cold before, now seems to be part of your hand, though of course it's not. It only seems that way. The music seems to be seeping into your dreams, even your waking dreams, and the edges of your vision have a haze you can't see through, which is probably good because something else is moving in this cellar and only the music keeps you protected.

You put down the key and stare at the new arrival, then the new arrivals, men and women and children arriving from someplace incomprehensible, all dressed in immaculate white robes that have somehow escaped the wet of the storm and the rot of the cellar. They're chanting, or humming, or in some way you can't quite grasp adding depth to the melody.

As long as the music plays, they cannot see you. If the music stops, their crimson eyes and sharpened teeth and claw-like fingernails will rend you apart.

But the key slips out of your hand.

It drops to the soft, soggy floor and sinks. You bend to retrieve it, before the music ends, but you can't dig through the dirt and you can't touch the key. It's like you've become insubstantial, not a part of the real world.

Frantically, you try to pick up the key. Failing that, you try to reclaim the music box. The rhythm falters, and the music dwindles until it's just individual notes, and the white-clad chanters drag you to one of the tables and tie tying you down with silken rope that bites through your otherwise unreal flesh.

You've transitioned into a ghostly form, and maybe you're already no longer alive, but the white-clad chanters have further plans for you. They draw your ghostly blood with needles until you've got nothing left to bleed, and they leave you helpless on the table as they drift away in the same ways they'd originally arrived. When none of them remain, and the last note has wrung free of the music box, the beast comes—a ghost-devouring beast that consumes what's left of your soul.

You chose poorly.

You turn around and run.

Right out of the police station, into the rain, into the storm. The policeman gives chase and is already radioing for assistance. Soon, there are flashing blue lights in every direction, and teams of officers combing the streets, and the old man outside Barlow's telling them how you seemed so fine and earnest.

You can't hide in the streets, and you can't find safe passage out of the town without being stopped by the police or the suddenly deputized townsfolk, so you climb the side of a brick building and hide on the rooftop.

From there, you have an excellent view of the police scattering in every direction, so very methodical, and you hear the officers reporting negative results here and there over the radio.

But eventually, someone sees your shadow and calls attention to it.

"There!" someone yells.

"The rooftops!" someone yells.

And as you try to flee, an overzealous cop, perhaps with a malicious streak but you'll never truly know, finds your heart with a single gunshot.

You chose poorly.

Although the alligators are tempting, you're not that foolhardy. You rush, instead, through the water, stepping behind the alligators to give them a fair amount of room.

One wrong step plunges you into an underwater hole. The swampy water grabs you and drags you under. Vines in the water tug at your legs and arms. You've lost your stick, and you can't break the surface to take a breath. You hear splashing, but it's probably not the alligators—it's probably just you.

Your next breath is actually a lungful of swamp, neither tasty nor rich in oxygen. You can't see, but you feel the big alligator's jaws closing on you, and you hear or imagine the swamp witch cackling behind you as you can't decide whether to drown first or be eaten.

Either way, the bog takes and keeps you, and you never reemerge from its waters.

You chose poorly.

"Of course I like you," you say. "I didn't mean anything by it."

"Do you mean it?"

"Yes."

"What do you like about me? Is it my eyes? I'm told my eyes sparkle."

"Yes, your eyes sparkle." You can't maneuver to the supply closet door and escape without squeezing past the nurse, which seems inadvisable. She's opening and closing her fists and staring down at your feet as she talks.

"And my voice? I ain't got the sound of a nightingale, I know that, but I've got a rather high soprano." She proves it with a quick *do re mi* to the top of her range.

"You have a lovely voice," you admit.

She looks up at you again, meets your eyes, and it's not a sparkle but a gleam you see there. She flings aside her second lollipop and advances on you again. This time, you don't resist, and before you know it she's kissing you and pulling you closer and wrapping you in her silken web. You try to resist, but she's stronger than you imagined. She lifts you bodily and attaches you to the corner of the ceiling, the small amount of webbing holding you in place.

Again, you try to struggle, but she's wrapping your legs and tying down your arms. She says, "I haven't had a snack in too long." Her mouth is watering, and her eyes are fragmented like a spider's—you hadn't seen that before, it wasn't visible before, they were blue but now they're not—and she's injected you with a paralyzing venom that's muting your senses and numbing your hands.

She saves you for a while, maybe three or four days, taking a chunk of flesh or a pint of blood when she wants it, doing other things, and finally, when she's had as much as she wants, she severs your head with her extra legs.

You chose poorly.

Returning to the foyer, you're faced with the stairs and the doorway again. A flash of lightning through the big window throws shadows across, and from, the chandelier. You're not entirely convinced you saw anything but the old iron and glass.

To ascend the stairs, go to Page 30.

To leave the house, go to Page 164.

To go through the doorway, go to Page 233.

There doesn't seem to be much to uncover, but you quickly realize this is a mistake. In the top drawer of the first sideboard, you find a selection of silver, forks and spoons and ladles and tongs for grabbing sugar and a variety of tools with uses beyond your experience. If that's real silver—and you have no reason to believe it's not—it's got to be worth a fortune.

Underneath, behind the doors, are a variety of serving bowls, candelabra and candlesticks, pitchers, and a variety of ornately designed centerpieces, the shapes of spiders and spider webs predominant.

You don't hear the door open, but you do hear the valet clearing his throat. "I should have known," he says. "A mere thief."

You turn to protest, but you turn just in time to see the machete coming down.

You chose poorly.

The music gets louder as you progress. It's tinny, all high pitches, like something from a music box rather than a record player. At the far end, the corridor turns ninety degrees to the right and the music is louder. Most definitely a music box of some sort. You step into what might be described as a room. The low ceiling is all wood beams and support structures for the old house above. Four tables occupy the room, wood picnic tables, all in sad shape, warped by time, dripping with black mold and lichen, supporting old oil lamps and candlesticks and an empty glass decanter, as well as one music box featuring a ballerina twirling as the music winds down to its conclusion.

The song sounds very familiar, but you can't place it. It sounds important. The music box's key is right there on the table next to it. If you want to wind it up and play the song again, go to Page 21.

If you would prefer to keep moving, go to Page 89.

The accusation is such a shock, you cannot even think. The police arrest you and fingerprint you and shoot your mugshots before taking your shoelaces and belt. All the while, he hurls a series of hateful comments: "I hope you rot." "What you did, it's inhumane and inhuman." "Something is seriously wrong with you."

Then, it's time for questions. Who are you? Where were you going? What were you doing? Did you argue? No? Are you sure? Why did your partner leave you and the safety of your car in your version of the story? What old house are you talking about? There's no such place outside the town line. Are you a storyteller? Why are you lying? What made you do it? How could you be so cruel?

You don't know how to answer most of the questions.

It's a long night, and in the morning you're taken, in handcuffs, to a courtroom. The judge sits behind a high bench and scowls down at you. Your defense attorney, whom you've never met, wears an ill-fitting suit. He says to the judge, "I object."

The judge says, "I don't care." The judge bangs his gavel a lot. The prosecutor presents a series of witnesses: the police officer first, of course, who has your fingerprints and your statement and your inability to flatly deny the charges.

"It's practically a confession," says the officer.

Then the old man is brought out, and he tells his story, which is something like what you remember but with added threatening gestures and ominous words. He does admit you'd paid for the beer, but then suggest it was to hide the fact that the rain hadn't quite washed all the blood off you yet.

You might ask what blood, but your attorney urges caution. "This isn't a trial," he tells you in a confidential whisper. "It's just an arraignment."

You tell him, "I never got a phone call."

"Of all the things to worry about, that should be the least of them. You're facing death, stranger, and justice in this town can be quick."

"You said it wasn't a trial."

John Urbancik

Your attorney makes a gesture that suggests maybe he did, maybe he didn't.

Finally, the judge asks how you plead. Your attorney suggests a guilty plea would probably not result in a death sentence.

If you would like to plead not guilty, go to Page 8.

If you would like to plead guilty, go to Page 81.

The dining table could easily sit twenty. There are, in fact, only five there now, sitting around what appears to be a grand display of meat. It's not cooked meat. The odor is rather foul, and you're not sure you want to know where it came from or what it was when it was alive.

You realize the smell isn't only coming from the meat on the table. The diners themselves are in various stages of rot, with wounds under their clothes that you didn't immediately notice, wounds still bloody or festering.

One looks up at you and says, quite distinctly, "*Brains.*"

They all look at you. They look hungry, even as they eat. But they are eating, and they're not making any move to involve you in any way.

If you prefer to go back through the kitchen and try the hall, go to Page 82.

If you would like to go back through the kitchen and into the walk-in freezer, go to Page 109.

You can try to go around them to the corridor visible at the far end. Go to Page 334.

The valet places a vinyl disc on the old Victrola The sound is scratchy and tinny, from before you were born—but maybe not before the Queen was born. She steps down from the throne as the music begins.

It's a tango.

The Queen, despite her age, is agile and quick, an excellent dance partner, far more skilled at the tango than you. She leads. If it weren't for the circumstances, it might be considered romantic. It probably *is* romantic, just not by the usual definition of the word.

When it's over, she whispers, "I wish you hadn't lied to me."

As she steps away, she gives the valet some sort of signal. It's all so fast, you don't even have time to react. He's there, with his machete, and the signal was some variation of *Off with his head.*

You chose poorly.

"Thanks, but no," you say.

The nurse narrows her eyes. "What, you think I'd poison the lollipops? Are you mad?"

"I have other things on my mind."

You're thinking, of course, of your lover, lost in the woods, and the old house outside of town, but the nurse lowers her voice to something almost comically femme fatale and curves her red lips into something resembling a smile. "I know."

She tosses the lollipop aside and steps toward you so quickly, you barely have time to react. You're already backed against the door and bang your head.

"Oh," she says, "have you got a booboo? I'm a genuine certified registered nurse, you know. I can help." Like a snake, her hand slides up toward the back of your head.

You tell her to stop, and she does. And she pouts. She pouts like a child being denied a cookie. "I thought you might be fun, but you're no fun at all." She turns abruptly and returns to the lollipops to fish out another. "Don't you like me?"

If you're not ready to admit you like the nurse, go to Page 42.

If you like the nurse, go to Page 62.

There must be a police station in this town. You walk its streets until you find one. It's not much of anything, just a window and a door in the very last building on the left. You can't see through the window, but you enter. Inside, you find regular real light to chase away the gloom, even if the light is pale and tinted slightly industrial in the way of fluorescents. There's a back area, but first there's a uniformed policeman sitting behind a large desk looking down at you. He asks, "What can I do for you?"

You tell him everything about the mysteriously dying car and your missing partner and the rain and the creature, the officer taking notes the entire time. When you're done, he looks up, and he says, "We've been looking for you. See, we've found your lover's body."

"What?"

"And the murder weapon."

You stare dumbly.

"We know you're guilty."

You have no response to this.

"Murderer."

Flee. Go to Page 60.

If you'd rather be arrested, go to Page 66.

It's a long hall with doors on either side. Behind you, the moaning of zombies resembles a chant of "Brains. Brains. Brains." When you try one of the doors, it resists for a moment, and finally opens.

Inside, zombies sit at a poker table in a whirl of cigar smoke. They turn at once and rise to come after you.

Slamming the door, you find more zombies in the next room, a bedroom, involved in some sort of orgy involving rotten body parts and things you'll wish you hadn't seen for the rest of your life. Disrupted, they turn their attention to you and extricate themselves from their various impossible positions and shamble toward the door.

Slamming it shut, you continue down the hall, followed now, chased, targeted, and you don't even try the next couple of doors because you expect the worst. They're opening anyway, because the noise of your flight and the undead pursuit, and zombies are emerging ahead of you as well as behind.

Finally, you find yourself surrounded.

And there's not much you can do. When running is no longer an option, you try to fight. Your fists aren't terrible weapons, but their dead bodies don't register the pain. Your nerve endings, however, light up with every scratch, tear, and bite.

Their sheer numbers overwhelm you.

You chose poorly.

Returning to the foyer, you're faced with the stairs and the den again. A flash of lightning through the big window throw shadows across, and from, the chandelier, though you're not entirely convinced you saw anything but the old iron and glass.

To ascend the stairs, go to Page 30.

You can leave the house. Go to Page 164.

Or go through the doorway, go to Page 233.

You leave town the way you came, up the same road, toward the house and your dead car and your lost lover. The woods are quiet around you, if the storm is tumultuous, and you're sure the creature shadows your every step.

It's a long walk, but the night seems entirely unchanged. The house remains ominous. The car remains lifeless. You didn't notice earlier, but there's also a church, hidden in the woods, only visible when you approach from this direction.

It's of the same kind of structure and material as the house, and looks no less promising. But it seems a more likely destination for your partner than a dark house in the middle of nowhere—admittedly, the church is also dark and in the middle of nowhere, but that's semantics.

> *You can return to the house, walk up to the front door and announce yourself. Go to Page 2.*
>
> *To sneak around the back of the house and climb in through a window, go to Page 3.*
>
> *You can enter the house through the cellar doors in the back. Go to Page 4.*
>
> *To explore the church, go to Page 9.*
>
> *You can wait in the front seat of your dead car as the red rain pummels its roof. If so, go to Page 10.*

You tell the Queen the quick version of the story: your dead car and mobile phone, the spooky house on the hill—you leave out that you climbed in through a window—and your missing lover.

The Queen listens intently. When you finish, she says, "Your story moves me. Victor, please, show our guest the way through."

The valet says, "Of course," and leads you to another door. He opens it for you and says, "Good luck."

You bow once more to the Queen, then step out of the throne room and back into the reality of a house on a hill. The hall is narrow and dimly lit, the carpet old, the odor stale and lifeless. When the valet pulls shut the door behind you, the throne room is completely and utterly gone. All that remains is a wall with dated, dingy wallpaper and possibly bloodstains.

The hall, in fact, is a landing, between a higher and lower floor. You can descend. Go to Page 147.

Or you can go up. Go to Page 243.

"Zombies!" you say. It's the first word, and the first breath, and you manage to get a grip on yourself. "Downstairs," you add.

She nods. "I know. That's why I'm up here. They're terrible at stairs." You don't answer immediately. As she descends from the ladder, she adds, "That's also why I'm in the library. Have you seen this?"

It's a book.

"No," you say.

"The title isn't Latin," she says. "It's older. I'm not sure what it is. But the words inside, there was a monk back in the seventeenth century who rewrote all the spells."

"Spells?"

"Specifically," she says, "I'm after the anti-zombie formula." She shakes the book like a prize. "And this, this is the book that's got it. Will you help me?"

Help her, go to Page 149

Don't help. Go to Page 189.

She gives you a needle. "I'm Shirley, by the way, and I've been working on this formula for seventy weeks. With you here, everything is finally in place."

You stick the tip of your finger. You let one drop of blood fall into her concoction. She does the same with another needle. "Can't risk infection," she says with a wink.

With a stone pestle, she crushes the collection of herbs and spices. "It's not so innocent as it looks," she tells you. "I wouldn't put this in my spaghetti sauce."

As she crushes and mixes everything together, it becomes like paste, green and unappetizing. You ask, "How does it work?"

She makes a face and puts down the pestle. "I'll have to ingest this. Then go down amid them and recite the spell."

"Will it work?"

"If it doesn't," Shirley tells you, "I die." Then, with her fingers, she pinches a bit of the mixture and puts it on her mouth. Her face contorts. "It's *terrible*," she says, then shovels more into her mouth.

The spell is written on a thick, yellowed piece of paper. She waves it as she leaves the room. "Hopefully, I'll be back in a minute."

Go forward and leave her to it. Go to Page 172.
Go with her to Page 178.

You take a breath but don't try to struggle. There are too many of them. They have you too tightly. The leader smiles as he recites ancient poetics, ritualistic words from lost tongues that suddenly have deep, tremendous meaning for you. You understand the names. You know the faces of the old gods, and you hear their heartbeats, and you feel their collective inhalation of anticipation as the knife comes down.

It pierces straight to your heart.

Death will come, but not so quickly as you might think. You have time to see the doors within your heart unfold and unlock and open. You witness the rise of the old gods, powerful and tremendous things apathetic to the plights of mankind. As they rise, they consume all the congregants. They consume all the townsfolk not hiding beneath hooded cloaks in a dingy basement room. They consume the residents of the old spooky house you had abandoned, and they consume your lost lover, whose fate you almost glimpsed. They consume the state and the region and the country and the continent, and they are freed to again sail across the blackness of space. Only once they have doused the sun and shattered the moon and launched themselves toward a particular star in a particular constellation—perhaps Altair, perhaps Vega, perhaps Sirius— you might have known, you probably did know—but only after they've taken to the celestial winds do you finally breathe your last.

You chose poorly.

You and the woman from the library run down the hall. It's a long hall with many doors. The first two are locked. The zombies are behind you.

And the zombies are ahead of you, rising from a staircase at the far end of the hall. The doors, even the locked doors, open from the inside to reveal even more of them. There must be hundreds in total. They're everywhere. They have you completely surrounded.

The woman takes your hand and squeezes and says, "I wish I'd never met you."

The press of zombies is too great to resist. They take the two of you down, they moan, they feast, they damage your bodies and kill you and turn you into the undead.

Briefly, you can see through your dead eyes, but all you see is hunger.

You chose poorly.

You take her hand. And now that you're close enough, now that it's too late, you can truly see her and smell her foul stench. She's a swamp witch, and she gives you the wickedest of grins as she pulls and says, "Out of the water, savior of mine."

The swamp witch pulls you onto the raft—and just in time, as the alligator is back and this time it's got friends. Another ten seconds, you would've felt its jaws.

"What did you expect, a princess?" the swamp witch asks. She's still got your hand. The raft, after teetering momentarily as you climbed aboard, settles. "Now tell me, what brings you to my swamp?"

If you want to tell her the truth, go to Page 97.

If you don't want to tell her, go to Page 150.

You stand before the judge and say, "If it pleases the court, I would like to enter a plea of guilty."

Your attorney jumps in with: "And beg both the court's compassion and leniency in sentencing."

"Fine," the judge says, banging his gavel and twirling it like a gunslinger. "The evidence is quite compelling, and the court accepts your plea of guilt. I sentence you to death by hanging."

You protest. Your attorney merely shakes his head. He says, "*C'est la vie.*"

"Aren't you going to appeal?" you ask.

"What for? You pled guilty The judge's word is law. It was nice knowing you, kid."

To await your fate, go to Page 36.

If you want to try to escape the courthouse, go to Page 316.

The hall is longer, maybe longer than the house, and though there are doors on one side, they're all locked. Behind you, there's the sound of chewing, a vicious and animal sound, so there's probably no going back.

Finally, the hall ends in a ballroom. A *Phantom of the Opera* chandelier hangs in the middle of a ballroom. And though the house was big from the outside, it seems like the room is at least as big as the house. There's a long bar along one side, with shelves full of bourbon and scotch and tequila. A bartender wipes clean one of the wine glasses, looking at you the whole time. When you finally look toward him, the bartender smiles, puts down the glass, and says, "What shall I get you?"

Be specific. Tell him what you want to drink. Go to Page 33.

Refuse the drink. Go to Page 182.

Ask for whatever's good. Go to Page 238.

The music gets quieter as you progress until, after a corner, you cannot hear it at all anymore. The corridor turns ninety degrees to the left.

There, you face an old door in old brick. There's an iron lock, but it's not engaged. You're able to push open the door. It creaks when you do so, and leads into a deeper darkness, an empty room. On one wall, there are empty wood shelves that have seen better days. Spiders crawl across them, and the splinters seem almost alive in the dim light behind you.

But there is light ahead, in the next room, and there you find a stone altar with archaic symbols scrawled on it. There are cuffs where ankles and wrists have been bound, though no sacrifice is there presently. A single bare bulb attempts to light this room but doesn't make a tremendous effort to do so. Propped against one wall so that you didn't immediately see it is a desiccated corpse. It's more dust than flesh now. Its eyes are empty sockets. Its blood had streaked the wall as it fell after the wound that shattered its chest like that, but the blood dried long ago and all that's left is a stain.

He blinks suddenly and looks at you without eyes and says, "Wanna dance?"

Retreat, go to Page 143.

Stand your ground, go to Page 228.

Run forward to the next room, go to Page 282.

You acknowledge the old man's toast, but you don't drink. Something about the beer is off, perhaps its fragrance. And the way the barkeeper looks at you, with hungry eyes, makes you hesitant.

"Will you make a man drink alone?" he asks.

You say, "Perhaps I should just go."

"And your belly all empty of beer," the old man says. "Fine. Go. Pay the barkeep, though, and be on your way."

If you pay the barkeep, go to Page 29.

If you'd prefer to leave without paying the barkeep, go to Page 203.

The old man sneers at you. "There's a bed at the inn, I'm sure."

"Where's that?"

He points behind you. "Big house in the woods, twenty minutes down the road."

You look behind you, beyond the creature and at the house you'd just left. Too late, you feel the old man's blade slip between your ribs. He whispers, "I don't much take to *cowards.*" He pulls back and stabs you again, and again, continuously and repeatedly, and there's nothing left for you to do but die.

You chose poorly.

You go through the left door into a sitting room. Chairs and couches fill the room. Candles burn on the surface of every side table. A variety of people sit throughout the room, though not every seat is occupied. Some of them look at you when you enter. Others pointedly do not.

"There's been a breach," one of the women tells you.

"A breach?"

"The portal is open. The demon emerges."

Everyone in the room repeats those last three words: "The demon emerges."

"Are you prepared?" one of the men asks.

If you don't think you are, go to Page 141.

If you think you're prepared, go to Page 194.

"You wanted rescuing," you tell her. "Come with me." You put out your own hand. You don't need to climb onto the raft. You need to get her off of it and out of the swamp.

"I can't leave," she tells you. And now that you're close enough, you can truly see her and smell her foul stench. She's a swamp witch, and she gives you the wickedest of grins. "But you were a doll to try."

If you wish to flee the swamp witch before she does anything, go to Page 48.

If you don't feel obliged to flee, go to Page 186.

The zombies reach for you and grab at you. You use your fists and all your martial arts skills, and you even use an unopened bottle of 25 year old Scotch. It doesn't break the first time you smash a zombie skull, but it shatters the second time, spilling all its contents and filling the air with a sweet, sticky smell.

But the zombies don't need weapons. The zombies don't feel pain, so none of your blows have any effect. When one of the zombies catches your arm, its grip is unbreakable. Sure, they move slowly, but they move relentlessly, and they relish fresh meat.

You've become zombie food. The bartender, looking on, shakes his head and continues cleaning his glasses. It's a long and ultimately pointless death.

You chose poorly.

Deeper into the cellar, you find the air thickens and the dirt ground becomes swampy, sucking at your shoes. The sounds of the storm are distant echoes now. Instead, you hear the sounds of the swamp: something sluicing through the boggy waters, the single flap of predatory wings as something launches after prey. You're not even sure you're in the cellar anymore, as the walls have moved from dark and dank through rotted and moldy into the black lichenous ichor of a dying swampland, more like bark than sheetrock, though you're still moving in a singular direction.

Finally, you break through the end of the path and find yourself at the edge of a treacherous lake. The surface is still and mirror-like, but dusted with scum and iridescence.

Fifty meters out, a woman sits on a chair on a raft. She wears wispy white and stares up at a moon that, though it shines on her, doesn't reach you. She sits facing away from you, but she turns and looks over her shoulder, and says, quite softly but somehow audibly, despite the distance, "Help me."

Help her. Go to Page 55.
Go back. Go to Page 151.

Every step creeks as you climb. The stairs look to be ancient, older than the house itself, and maybe they are. At the top, a thin door leads into a small kitchen. There's a stovetop and an oven, a refrigerator, and a man seated at a table. The man sits with his eyes closed, his hands on the table and palms up. A candle burns next to him.

He says, without opening his eyes, "I've been expecting you."

"Have you?" you ask.

"You are a seeker," the man says. "Tonight, at least, it's not something so esoteric as enlightenment. You seek a friend. A companion. No, a lover." He opens his eyes. They're all white, not a shred of color, not a black dot of pupil. "Answer my riddle, and I will tell you which way to go."

There are, in fact, two choices, a door to the left and a door to the right.

Go to the left door. Page 86.

Attempt to answer the riddle. Go to Page 196.

Go to the right door. Page 200.

You struggle against the arms that hold you, but by now the entire congregation has gotten out of their chairs and closed in around you. The all want to touch you, to hold you down, to keep you still. Their leader raises a ceremonial knife and offers thanks to gods whose names you can't comprehend.

He recites ancient poetics, ritualistic words from lost tongues that suddenly have deep, tremendous meaning for you. You understand the names. You know the faces of the old gods, you hear their heartbeats, and you feel their collective inhalation of anticipation as the knife comes down.

It pierces straight to your heart.

Death will come, but not so quickly as you might think. You have time to see the doors within your heart unfold and unlock and open. You witness the rise of the old gods, powerful and tremendous things apathetic to the plights of mankind. As they rise, they consume all the congregants. They consume all the townsfolk not hiding beneath hooded cloaks in a dingy basement room. They consume the residents of the old spooky house you had abandoned, and they consume your lost lover, whose fate you almost glimpsed. They consume the state and the region and the country and the continent, and they are freed to again sail across the blackness of space. Only once they have doused the sun and shattered the moon and launched themselves toward a particular star in a particular constellation—perhaps Altair, perhaps Vega, perhaps Sirius— you might have known, you probably did know—but only after they've taken to the celestial winds do you finally breathe your last.

You chose poorly.

You clear your throat. "Excuse me," you say. "I don't mean to interrupt, but..."

The pianist turns her head first. She stares straight at you with dead, jaundiced eyes. The wounds on her face are not fresh, but the decay is. When she stops with the keys, the audience seems to come to life—which is a misnomer—lifting themselves from their chairs and couches, turning their gazes at you, each revealing a more horrifying visage than the last. They're dead, all of them, dead and decaying, some fresh enough for maggots and worms to still be wriggling in their flesh.

They moan. They groan. They whimper. One manages a word: "Brains?" It sounds like a question. You don't know who they're asking.

They came to life with the cessation of the music. If you think hitting the keys will settle them back down, go to Page 128.

If you prefer to run, go to Page 202.

"If it's alright with you," you say, "I appreciate the last minute rescue, but I still have to save my partner."

"I understand," the doctor says. "If I were you, I'd do the same." He ushers you back toward the door, but at the last minute jabs you in the shoulder with a syringe. "I'm sorry it won't work out that way. You know how it is, right?"

The room sways. You have no chance to even consider an answer.

When you wake, you're tied to a table. Leather straps hold your wrists, your legs, your chest. A quick test of their strength assures you there'll be no easy escape.

The doctor, beside you, says, "Ah, you're awake. I expected the anesthesia to keep you under for longer, but one can never be too careful." He lifts a scalpel, contemplates it a moment, then sets it back on his tray of surgical tools. "That won't do at all, will it? I mean, we really need to open you up, don't we? How else will we find out what went wrong?"

He goes to the side of the room. You try to say something, but a tube stuffed down your throat prevents all but grunts and similar noises.

"Now, now," the doctor says, "I'm sure there's no need for such language." He returns with a bone saw. With the press of a button, he starts the blade spinning. It sounds like a dentist's drill, though it won't be nearly so pleasant.

As to anesthesia, there's no trace of it in your veins, so you feel every cut, with the bone saw and the bone chisel, clamps and mallets, scissors and hooks and lancets, and finally the rib spreader.

The operation lasts longer than you do.

You chose poorly.

The aliens leave. The day stretches infinitely until the next night, and the night is just as long. They days and nights grow longer and longer, and surely you should already be dead from lack of food and dehydration. At some point, you're no longer able to sit up, and you're no longer able to close your eyes, and even if someone entered the jail cell with bread and wine, you would be unable to eat.

More days pass until finally, mercifully, your consciousness fades, and you pass from this life.

You chose poorly.

The zombie doesn't race after you. Either it's slow, or it's perfectly content eating rancid meat in the malfunctioning freezer.

Go to Page 307.

You run back the way you came, toward the hall, and manage to round the corner just as the bartender lets loose his first shot. You feel the wind of the blast behind you.

Ahead of you, however, a group of zombies lumber toward you. They're messy and bloody and raw, and they're hungry. Seeing you, they increase their speed, though they're still moving slowly.

Stand and fight, go to Page 41.

Run back toward the bar in the ballroom, go to Page 191.

You tell the witch everything—almost everything—from your dying car and the useless mobile phone to your missing lover and the spooky house on the hill—though you leave out sneaking in through the cellar door. As you tell your story, she listens intently.

Finally, she says, "Your story moves me." She nods once, then again, as though considering something in her head. "I intended to feed you to the swamp, but I once believed in something very much like love, so I'll send you back."

She snaps her fingers, and a green twinkling light—a firefly, maybe?—whizzes through the cypresses, right past your ear, to hover in front of her sounding very much like a hummingbird. "This is a wisp," she says, "which are generally unreliable, but this one—forget her name, it doesn't matter to you—she'll guide you true."

The wisp takes off, passing the other side of your head. When you turn to see where it's gone to, it's bouncing around about twenty yards deep into the swamp. You tell her thanks. Turning away and nearly mumbling, the swamp witch says, "Go, before I change my mind."

The wisp zips forward twenty and thirty feet at a time. You have to move quickly to keep up, though the swamp does everything it can to slow you down. The roots of trees try to trip you, the limbs grab at you from above, a swarm of mosquitos dive bomb you as you move. The trees are giving way to cellar walls again, until they're not, and the wisp may be leading you somewhere but you can't be sure where.

Continue following the wisp, go to Page 127.
Try to get back on your own. Go to Page 155.

The window does not open noiselessly, but it does open. The big man probably had already seen you anyway. It's a smallish window, just big enough for you to squeeze through, so maybe the big guy won't be able to chase you out here.

Out here, however, is a slick, slippery, tiled mess. The rain pummels you. Lightning dances all around. Thunder overwhelms any other sounds. The roof's slope is rather steep here, but it's entirely uneven, and there are enough flat sections that you're able to put some distance between you and the window.

It's like the surface of the roof, now that you're on it, has nothing in common with the roofline you'd seen from the ground, though admittedly you hadn't actually studied it. There are outcroppings and other windows—all locked, and all too dark to reveal anything inside. There are gargoyles and weather vanes and chimneys and pipes. Graffiti in a variety of languages suggest you're not the first person.

When you look back, the big man has stuck his head out the window and leers at you. He ducks back in. A moment later, a child hops out, a child with infinitely more agility than you, a child without fear of the rain-slicked rooftop. A second such child follows. One boy, one girl, they look at you with the same hungry eyes as the big man, presumably their father. They carry straight razors like claws.

There's no place to hide. Do you want to abandon caution and run in hopes of finding an open window? Go to Page 117.

Would you prefer to proceed cautiously, knowing the children will probably catch up to you pretty quickly? Go to Page 135.

Or stand and defend yourself. Go to Page 174.

"Sorry, I don't have anything," you tell her.

"That's okay," she says. "I have very particular dietary needs."

The way she says it makes you nervous. "I'm sure Rebecca will be along soon," you say.

"She's here every night."

You tell her, "The night's still young. But I better be going."

"Goodnight," she tells you. "I hope you find what you're looking for."

You never see the woman behind the curtain, which may be a good thing. Through her room, you enter another chamber, a massive room with couches, a fireplace and mantle, and a number of books.

To explore the room, go to Page 113.

To continue on to the next room, go to Page 223.

You try to escape the falling statue, but another comes from another direction. One pushes you into the path of the other, and the other crushes you like a bug. Bones break. The chandelier light goes out, burying you into darkness. You cannot move, trapped as you are. Your leg might be broken, and also your ribs. Everything hurts.

Revealed by the light of a torrent of lightning, a final statue falls toward you and shatters your skull.

You chose poorly.

Into the library, you slam the door shut behind you.

"What did you *do* down there?" the woman demands. But you don't have an answer. She's rifling through the books, throwing them aside randomly, searching for something but you have no idea what.

"What do we do?" you ask.

Finally, she finds what she was looking for, a leather-bound text with a fancy calligraphy on its spine that reads *Undead.*

"What kind of library is this?" you ask.

She ignores your question, drops the big book on one of the tables, and flips through pages. "There's got to be something on eradication," she says.

The zombies are at the door. It's a solid door. Strong wood. Old and sturdy. But you can feel it giving in under the press of the undead outside it. You shove a table against it, which takes effort, as though that might give you any extra hope of survival.

"*Control,*" she says. "I can't destroy them, but I *can* direct them."

"How?"

"A spell," she says. "It requires...it requires spices, blood, lizard bits, and the venom of a black widow."

"Do you happen to have any of that here in this library?" you ask.

"Actually," she says, "yes. You have to do something."

Refuse. Go to Page 132.

Do what she says, go to Page 197.

The old man laughs. "I like your pluck, "he says, slapping his knee. "Your lover is lost, possibly dead, maybe being tortured to death right now at Old Coop's Mansion, and you think you can wash away your troubles with a fine stout."

He drags himself out of the rocking chair. It's a slow, arduous, rickety motion, and it seems to take effort. If you offer to help, he ignores it. He eventually reaches his feet and leans close enough to whisper, "I reckon there's a beer or two to be had down at Barlow's, if you've got a dollar to buy an old man a drink."

He leads you to the place. The entrance is in one of the brief alleys, steps below street level and into a dimly lit tavern with a lot of wood and hunting trophies—deer and elk heads and the like—on the walls. The woman behind the bar nods at the old man and draws two drinks into solid glass steins. The old man laughs the whole time, talking about how the town's been around since the dawn of something, there's always been strangers and they've always been welcomed, and so many end up staying not just for the rest of their lives but forever.

The woman serves two beers. The old man takes his, says, "To a dish fit for king," and drinks.

If you drink, go to Page 39.

If you don't drink, go to Page 84.

The zombie reaches for you and grabs at you. You use your fists and all your martial arts skills, and you even use a can of something as a weapon.

But the zombie doesn't need weapons. The zombie doesn't feel pain, so none of your blows have any effect. When the zombie catches your arm, its grip is unbreakable. Sure, it moves slowly, but it moves relentlessly, and it relishes fresh meat.

You've become zombie food. It's a long, frigid, and ultimately pointless death.

You chose poorly.

You flee, back the way you came, before too many of the dead dancers are aware of you, but the hall is occupied by fresh arrivals—freshly dead arrivals, additional zombies oozing blood and pus and death. They don't start moaning until they see you. The fresh zombies reach for you from the hall, the dancers reach for you from behind. Together, they overpower you, they drag you down to the ground, and they sate their hunger for flesh and brains.

You chose poorly.

"Wait." Your voice is hoarse from lack of use, but it's enough to stop the aliens from simply abandoning you. Hallucinations or not, they're the only thing that can break you out of this cell. "Let me free."

The aliens confer in their alien language noises. Finally, one of them touches the lock on the cell. The mechanism clicks open. The aliens leave before you can thank them. It's an effort to stand, to follow them out of the jailhouse. The police officer is nowhere to be seen. Out on the streets, you find dust. The trees that aren't already skeletal cling only to crisp brown leaves. The grass crunches under your feet as you stumble through the few patches of it.

You wander for a good long while, finding nothing and no one, and ultimately settle on a bench alongside the main road through town. A folded newspaper lies at the top of the adjacent trashcan. The headline is blatant: *Earth Dries Up, Aliens to Blame.* You can't read the story itself. The words are an illegible jumble of blurry inkblots.

You see the alien ship leave the earth. It's bright like a comet, and takes most of five minutes to rise out of the atmosphere.

You wander—perhaps for days, perhaps weeks, perhaps merely hours—but you're alone on the earth, the sole survivor, left for reasons you may never comprehend, but you aren't long for it. Without water, without food, you don't survive much longer.

You chose poorly.

Avoiding the mirror, you say, "Hello," and tell the valet your name. He rises, and says, "I'll inquire as to whether or not the Queen is presently receiving visitors."

The valet is only gone a minute or so before returning. "The Queen," he says, "will receive you." He holds open the door.

You step into the Queen's room.

It's enormous. You could fit entire houses in this one room. The ceiling is two or three stories high, the numerous windows just as tall, with wallpaper out of the eighteenth century, as though you've stepped into a throne room of some ancient European palace.

Marble statues adorned with gold represent all twelve gods of the Greek pantheon. The chandelier, made up of a thousand and one candles, throws flickering light everywhere, reflecting off the crystals hanging there—possibly emeralds and rubies and sapphires—casting infinite shades of color throughout the room.

The cleanest, brightest light falls on the Queen herself. She sits on one of two thrones, red velour lined with gold, equal in size and stature. The other seat is dusty, coated in cobwebs, but the rest of the room is immaculate and wonderful and overwhelming.

It's almost enough to make you forget everything.

And the Queen herself: she sits on her throne in a lake of crimson fabric, complex lacework and brocades, silver around her neck and hanging from her ears and in her fingers. She holds a scepter, wields it, really, as though it's a weapon. With it, she motions you to the center of the room, where all eyes of the court would be looking—but you're alone in this throne room with the Queen and her valet.

You step to the center of the room, and bow as best you can before her royal highness. She laughs. "Rise, child, and tell me who you are and what you want."

Lifting your head, you realize the Queen is in fact ancient—beautiful, yes, but it's not the beauty of youth that radiates from her. She's as dusty and web-filled as the empty throne beside her, her eyes the palest you've ever seen, and the silver spider hanging from a chain over her décolletage almost looks alive.

Tell her the truth. Go to Page 130.
Tell her something else. Go to Page 165.

The wisp leads you deeper into the swamp, until it's leading you deeper into the cellar—or a cellar, maybe not the same one—and then through the swamp again. The trees are unnatural, the moonlight is fading, the sounds of a distant thunderstorm never come closer but never fade away.

"Where are you taking me?" you ask.

The wisp doesn't answer. The wisp merely continues to lead you further and further astray. When you finally realize you're not making any real progress, that maybe you're going around in circles, you also realize you're not alone. The wisp has gone beyond sight, but between trees you see the vaguely human eyes of an enormous skunk ape toward your left, and another, shorter and stockier, to your right. At least half a dozen of them surround you before you even know they're there, and now they're inescapable.

They're huge, the smallest of them still twice your weight and half again your height, and they're solid muscle under all that fur. They've been hunting, but the hunt is over because in another moment they've not merely surrounded but captured their prey—you—their next meal.

It does not end prettily. Skunk apes are notoriously messy eaters.

You chose poorly.

You pull open the freezer door, but it's warmer inside than you think it should be and a shallow puddle covers the floor. There are boxes on aluminum shelves, and plenty of cans, but if they were once neatly stacked, that's no longer the case. They've been upset and scattered and broken. Dead peas are strewn across the floor, asparagus sticks, and chunks of meat that have been thoroughly torn apart and partly devoured.

One of those bits of meat turns its head to look up at you. It's got fresh meat hanging from its jaw, fresh blood, and yellowed skin. The zombie grunts, and rises, and reaches for you.

Flee through the kitchen into the dining room, go to Page 95.

Stand and fight, go to Page 103.

Flee through the kitchen down the hall, go to Page 118.

Looking around at the expanding menagerie, you tell the green-eyed woman about your dead car and useless phone, and about the disappearance of your partner and lover.

"Then we shall find your lover," the woman says. She steps forward and wraps an arm around you to pull you close. For a moment, you think she's going to kiss you—you're not quite sure how that would work—but that's not it at all. She lifts you off the grated iron walkway around the library and floats into the air above the room of dolls.

Then the other creatures, two dozen of them or more, attack the house in every direction. They tear into the walls and rip through the ceiling. You hear glass shattering, now that the thunder has paused, and you hear things crashing through floors. Something splashes, and apparently a fight of some sort ensues on the shore of a lake hidden within the house—it makes no sense to you, all the noises, the screams of ghosts being torn asunder, ghouls shrieking in terror, church bells going mad. Right down the middle, the house cracks. The crack expands and widens and shatters everything in its path.

The creatures ravage the house. Windows shatter. Rooms collapse. Fires erupt. The night sky breaks open like a spider's web. The house comes tumbling down, with the woods around it, a church, a town.

The woman gently lands you in a clear spot at the center of this unnatural storm. In the end, not a single wall of the house remains standing. There are bodies, too many bodies to count, some of them grotesque things you've never imagined. The creatures of the *Bestiarum Vocabulum* scatter into the night, leaving you alone amid the ruins.

From the smoldering ruins, a single figure emerges, growing more distinct with every step: your lover. The green-eyed woman says, "Thank you," then rises into the air like a missile—and you don't want to know where she's headed. The wax burns under your fingernails.

It's morning, and the first weak light of dawn strains to break through the clouds. Reunited, you and your partner return to the car where you left it, and it starts right up. You and your lover drive away from the ruins of the spooky old house on the hill.

Congratulations. You chose well.

Meeting the guest of honor sounds like too exciting an opportunity to pass up.

"Great," the bartender says, grinning, putting down his cloth. "This way."

He triggers a release to open a door in the back of the bar. A panel of wine and whiskey swings back to reveal a hidden staircase. The secret door swings shut behind you as you ascend.

"She's a genuine treasure," the bartender says. "Old friend of the family. In her home country, she's royalty."

"A princess?" you ask.

At the top of the stairs, there's a door, which the bartender opens and allows you to enter first. As you're walking in, he says, "No, not a princess. A *queen*."

In this anteroom, a perfectly groomed man in full white tie regalia sits with his fingers splayed in front of his face. He's staring at himself in a mirror. The room is larger than it needs to be, occupied only by that one chair—which is extravagant—thick wood sideboards on either side, and the big, ornate mirror.

"A guest," the bartender says, as way of announcement, "to see the Queen."

The valet, still staring into the mirror, says, "Splendid."

Meet the valet's eyes in the mirror, go to Page 23.

Greet the valet to his back, go to Page 106.

The books are grimoires, natural sciences, histories, and bestiaries, old and dusted, untouched in ages. When you touch one, something behind it moves. A spider, no bigger than your thumbnail, scurries into a deeper hiding place.

There's a desk with an open ledger filled with numbers and notifications, an inkwell, and a quill.

When you approach the fireplace and all the objects on its mantle—a sextet, a compass, a stuffed raven, a smooth black stone, two jars probably containing ink, a vial that may be poison but is probably—you hope—perfume, a small doll shaped vaguely like a person with button eyes and a mouth stitched shut.

There's also a human skull.

That's about all you need, don't you think? There's no one here, no sign of your lost lover, no explanation for your dead car or mobile phone, and nothing to learn. There are only the spiders—a dozen of them, now, emerging from behind the various oddments on the mantle.

One leaps at you.

Two leap at you.

They're behind you, too, and these aren't so small, some the size of a quarter or a half dollar, some even bigger. More pour through the fireplace, flowing down the chimney, these the size of your fist or your forearm or your face.

They're biting you and tying you with silk webbing. They're draining you of blood and filling you with venom. You fight back, squashing five or ten with swift swats of the hand. You probably crush some when you go down.

But the weight of them is more than you can bear. The number of them is impossible. They come from everywhere now, all around, every corner and crack of the room, and it's not long before they've got you pinned to the floor. You can't rise. The strands of web are too strong and too numerous.

You die slowly and in great agony.

You chose poorly.

Your awareness continues for quite a while even as your essence is diluted. Eventually, the swamp witch gathers the bits of you in a cauldron and makes a stew.

You chose poorly.

You brace yourself for the imminent attack. Your muscles are ready, your fight or flight response has been activated, but the valet makes no move to attack. "You want to meet the Queen, I take it?" he says.

You nod meekly. "Yes."

"I'll inform her highness you're seeking an audience."

He knocks on the big wooden doors, waits a respectable three count, then opens the door—just enough to slip past—and enters, leaving you briefly alone in the inverted anteroom. Here, the sideboards have shifted, and there's no bartender standing at the doorway leading down to, presumably, another ballroom.

Do you want to explore more before the valet returns? Go to Page 64.

If you wish to wait patiently and respectively, go to Page 249.

The table holds secrets, and it takes only a few seconds to find the release that opens its hidden door. You see something inside—you're not quite sure what, but you never have a chance to see it.

The thing under the stairs—a corpse or a ghoul crawling from death itself—grabs you from behind. The stink of it rushes in, overwhelming your senses. Its bear hug tightens. You can barely pull in breath. Ribs crack and snap under its strength. You try to resist, but it's like fighting steel with paper balls. The thing crushes you, and keeps crushing, squeezing until ribs and sternum and spine crack, until your skin splits, until your insides burst through the seams.

You chose poorly.

Maybe it's your shoes, or the surface of the rooftop, or just the heavy rainfall. Maybe it's an edge of panic. Whatever it is, you take off at a run and your second step slips right out from under you. You crash hard on your knee, slam your forearms against the solid tiles, and slide down the side of the roof.

You crash into another flat section, but so heavily you go right through it. A moment later, you're tumbling through the air, off the edge of the roof and down the side of the house.

It's only three stories. You might survive if you don't crash headfirst into something.

You land flat on your back. Bones crack. Pain erupts throughout your body. The children's faces peer over the edge of the rooftop. You're not dead, not yet, but you're not sure you can regain your feet or your breath any time soon.

The children hop off the edge of the roof. They land on either side of you, perfect superhero landings, razors still in hand. They can't be more than eight years old each, but they're also timeless, ancient, as though they'd been this age for centuries. They're swift with those razors, and they carve your life and soul from your flesh.

You chose poorly.

The zombie doesn't race after you. Either it's slow, or it's perfectly content eating rancid meat in the malfunctioning freezer.

Go to Page 82.

The two of you dance to the music of a zombie orchestra. The creatures even give you a minute, which is kind if perplexing, but soon enough your waltz is interrupted by the hungry horde. They tear the two of you apart violently and messily.

You chose poorly.

You recite a poem. It's not one of yours. Something old, something gothic, probably from the pen and mind of Edgar Allan Poe. It's the first poem that comes to mind, and one of the few you've memorized.

"That," the bartender/madman says, "was beautiful. I knew a poem once. It starts, *The world is a shadow of death.* Or is it *Death is a shadow of the world?* I forget. Sometimes, I'm easily confused." He pours another glass of absinthe, prepares another cube of sugar.

A green snake curls out of the glass. It's a small snake, smaller than a garden snake, but it grows as it slithers up and out. It swallows the sugar cube, then looks at you and asks, in an Eastern European tongue you shouldn't be able to understand, "Who's mad now?"

The hallucinatory snake strikes. The bartender/madman grins and begins to wipe down the bar. "Anyway," he says, as the snake's venom or the poison of the absinthe or both work quickly to boil your blood, "I'm always pleased to meet a poetic soul."

A fairy sits perched on his shoulder. She's green, like the absinthe, and beautiful, though tiny. She's shaking her head, and smiling for you, and she's the last thing you see before your tainted blood dissipates and oxygen fails to reach your vital organs.

You die with the hallucination of a snake clinging to your chest.

You chose poorly.

"I can answer one question," the old man tells you.

"Which door should I pick?"

He shakes his head. "I do not know."

"What do you know?"

"You've already asked your one question."

"You didn't have an answer to give me. You didn't say I can ask one question, you said you could answer one."

He smiles. It takes effort to lift his sagging skin. "You're right, at that. Okay, one door leads to your heart's desire. The other to a horrible death. I can give no indication. I cannot point to the right or tell you to avoid the left. I can only tell you there's a choice to be made, and you must make it, and I trust you won't choose poorly."

Choose the left door. Go to Page 139.

Choose the right door. Go to Page 247.

The valet places a vinyl disc on the old Victrola. The sound is scratchy and tinny, from before you were born—but maybe not before the Queen was born. She steps down from the throne as the music begins.

It's a tango.

The Queen, despite her age, is agile and quick, an excellent dance partner, far more skilled at the tango than you. She leads. If it weren't for the circumstances, it might be considered romantic. It probably *is* romantic, just not by the usual definition of the word.

When it's over, she whispers, "I wish you hadn't lied to me."

As she steps away, she gives the valet some sort of signal. It's all so fast, you don't even have time to react. He's there, with a machete he got from who knows where. The signal had been some variation of *Off with his head.*

You chose poorly.

You came in through the cellar, and you're still convinced it contains answers.

The corridor brings you to a large room, at the center of which is an altar, complete with inverted cross and a chalice full of wine. There are plenty of places to sit or kneel, but there's no one here. There's a book on the altar, something like a Bible but very much different.

If you want to look at the book, go to Page 134.
If you want to drink the wine, go to Page 279.

Through the red door with the blue sign that says "Madman", a small corridor leads you to the kind of bar that might be squeezed into a corner of an attic, which is exactly what it is.

The bartender is already pouring you a green drink. There's room for maybe one other person, but there's no one there. He sets a spoon atop the small glass, uses tongs to add a sugar cube, then pours ice water into the absinthe. He pushes the drink toward you and asks, "Are you a poet or a thief?"

Answer thief, go to Page 133.

Answer poet, go to Page 154.

Drink the absinthe and give another answer, go to Page 175.

Don't drink the absinthe or answer the question, go to Page 204.

Drink the absinthe and give no answer, go to Page 224.

The bartender shrugs. "Suit yourself." He returns to drying freshly cleaned glasses in anticipation of the dance. "Oh, look at that," he says, glancing toward the door you'd entered through. "You've brought company."

Zombies are pushing through the door, struggling to get past each other and the jamb. In various states of decay, they ooze and moan, and they move haphazardly.

"This," the bartender says, "doesn't look good." He nods toward another hall. "I recommend the stairs."

Stand and fight. Go to Page 88.

Take the bartender's advice and go to Page 129.

You continue toward the end of the room. There's a final window at the far end, open, this one overlooking the family cemetery. Figures drift among the stones, but they seem distant and gray under the thunderstorm.

"Oh, look," a voice behind you says, "you've had a *visitor.*"

When you turn, there's a man, easily a foot taller than you, broad and muscular, in a freshly reddened butcher's apron, looking down at the man chained to the bed. "Whatever shall we do?"

There's no other doors this way, no stairs, and no place to hide. If you want to risk the window, go to Page 98.

If you want to hold your ground, go to Page 173.

The wisp leads you deeper into the swamp, until it's leading you deeper into the cellar—or a cellar, maybe not the same one—and then through the swamp again. The trees are unnatural, the moonlight is fading, the sounds of a distant thunderstorm never come closer but never fade away.

"Where are you taking me?" you ask.

The wisp doesn't answer. The wisp merely continues to lead you further and further astray. When you finally realize you're not making any real progress, that maybe you're going around in circles, you realize you're no longer alone. The wisp has gone beyond sight, but between trees you see the vaguely human eyes of a skunk ape toward your left, and another, this one shorter and stockier, to your right. At least half a dozen of them surround you before you even know they're there, and now they're inescapable.

They're enormous, the smallest of them still twice your weight and half again your height, and they're solid muscle under all that fur. They've been hunting, but the hunt is over. The biggest of them carries its prey on its back. They pause to watch you.

A moment later, the wisp returns, buzzing and whizzing, frantically zipping this way and that, until you follow again.

When the bark on the cypresses fades back to something more solid, more like sheetrock or drywall or plaster or plywood, albeit covered with lichen and mucus and mold, you realize you've returned to the cellar, and the wisp disappears.

You might not be in the same place you left the cellar. You're not sure. It was all dark, dank corridors. The swampy ground has been replaced, and the sounds of the storm—still distant, yes—are no longer a world away.

But there are stairs, presumably up to the house. If you'd prefer to ascend, go to Page 90.

You can continue deeper into the cellar. If so, go to Page 123.

It's only a quick two steps to the piano, and you jab the first key you can reach. Doesn't matter which. The sounds kept the zombies complacent before you said anything, the notes will do the same now.

Except they don't. The pianist grabs your wrist as you're hitting keys. The pianist had been the only one moving before, so it makes sense, if you want to apply any sort of logic to the situation.

The zombie's grip is strong.

Whether the music calmed the zombie audience or not, you'll never know, because the music doesn't continue and they're on you in a matter of seconds. Trying to pull away from the pianist, you almost escape, but they're behind you as well, and they're not just hands, they're teeth, and they're tearing into you as though they've not ever eaten before.

You chose poorly.

You climb the wide, carpeted stairs to a landing which allows you to go either left or right.

To the right, there's a hall. Go to Page 131.

To the left, there's a doorway apparently leading to a library. Go to Page 180.

You tell the Queen the quick version of the story: your dead car and mobile phone, the spooky house on the hill—you leave out that you climbed in through a window—and your missing lover.

The Queen listens intently. When you finish, she says, "Your story moves me. Victor, please, show our guest the way through."

The valet says, "Of course," and leads you to another door. He opens it for you and says, "Good luck."

You bow once more to the Queen, then step out of the throne room and back into the reality of a house on a hill. The hall is narrow and dimly lit, the carpet old, the odor stale and lifeless. When the valet pulls shut the door behind you, the throne room is completely and utterly gone. All that remains is a wall with dated, dingy wallpaper and possibly bloodstains.

The hall, in fact, is a landing, between a higher and lower floor. You can descend. Go to Page 147.

Or you can go up. Go to Page 243.

It's a long hall with doors on either side. When you try the first door you reach, it resists for a moment, and finally opens. Inside, corpses sit at a poker table in a whirl of cigar smoke. They turn at once and rise and come after you.

Slamming the door, you find more undead in the next room, a bedroom, involved in some sort of orgy involving rotten body parts and things you'll wish you hadn't seen for the rest of your life. Disrupted, they turn their attention to you and extricate themselves from their various impossible positions and shamble toward the door.

Slamming it shut, you continue down the hall, followed now, chased, targeted, and you don't even try the next couple of doors because you expect the worst. They're opening anyway, because the noise of your flight and the undead pursuit, and zombies are emerging ahead of you as well as behind.

Finally, you find yourself surrounded.

And there's not much you can do. When running is no longer an option, you try to fight. Your fists aren't terrible weapons, but their dead bodies don't register the pain. Your nerve endings, however, light up with every scratch, tear, and bite.

Their sheer numbers overwhelm you.

You chose poorly.

She tells you what you have to do, how you have to entice a spidery woman to bite you and inject you with her venom.

"Um...no," you say.

And you're unwavering on that point.

"Fine," she says. "I'll do it."

She disappears through the other door—the library has only the two, and you hadn't even noticed the second because it was hidden behind shelves.

The zombies continue to press on the other door. It bends to the weight of them.

A long minute passes. The hall door cracks audibly. It won't last long.

Another long minute stretches toward two. The door behind you breaks. Arms burst through the splintered wood. They push the door forward, slowly, despite the table blocking it.

Just then, the other door opens. You expect to see the woman again, though you're not sure of the state of her. Instead, there's someone else, someone with extra arms and extra legs and long black hair and fresh blood dripping from her mouth.

Behind her, another just like her clings to the ceiling.

"Ah," the higher one says. "Dinner."

The spider women take you. When they bite, the venom paralyzes you almost immediately. They close the door behind them and lock it down with a good deal of webbing before taking you through to a bedroom. Here, tied by web to one of the posts of the four poster bed, the woman from the library hangs limply. She's tightly bound, and also paralyzed, but also drained of much of her blood.

The spider women bind your legs and arms, and attach you to one of the other posts, positioning you to stare straight at the woman from the library. She's not dead, you see that now, but she's close to it.

"Thief," you say, throwing back the absinthe like a champion.

As you put the glass down on the bar, the bartender catches your wrist. "I'm the madman," he says, lifting a machete from underneath the bar, "and I don't much appreciate thieves."

His grip is iron, and it only needs to be for the two seconds it takes him to lift the long, thick blade and bring it down. It cuts cleanly through the flesh and bone of your wrist and chips the wood of the bar.

"That's the proper way of dealing with thieves," the bartender/madman says.

Blood and shock precede the pain, but the pain comes and obscures everything. He's telling you something else now, something all friendly, about a recent guest here at the bar, and how he believes you may know each other, but it's too late for the both of you now because justice is swift.

As he speaks, your vision wavers and your strength fades as your blood attempts to escape through your severed wrist. You can't even look at it. It doesn't take long for the pain to fade, or for the world to go dark, and it doesn't take long for you to bleed out on the floor of an improbable attic bar.

You chose poorly.

It's an old book, dry leather that creaks when you touch it. The pages are thin, the writing in it ornate, the illustrations immaculate. But you can make no sense of it. The letters themselves are unlike anything you're familiar with. Certainly, they say something, but there's nothing you can recognize. The beasts in the illustrations are nonsensical, amalgamations of animals you know—spiders with the heads of queens, lions with eagle's claws, snakes with wings.

Whatever secrets the book contains, it reveals none of them to you.

Maybe you should go back to the stairs and rise out of the cellar. Go to Page 90.

Maybe you should try the wine. Go to Page 279.

You're not stupid enough to run, and luck is on your side. The next window is open, if just a crack, but you're able to muscle it up and slip in. You scrape your back getting in, and you almost get stuck, but you manage it before the children and their straight razors reach you. You slam the window shut again, and turn to flee into the house.

But you're still in the attic, and you're on the other side of the bed with the dismembered man on it. He's laughing. It's not a sane laugh.

The big man, still at the other window, looks at you and smiles. It's not a sane smile.

The woman, the mother of this cannibal family, blocks the doorway. Maybe you can get past her.

Arms emerge from under the bed like tentacles, and another victim, without legs, wraps up your feet. It takes only a moment to kick free, but that's all the woman and man need to reach you She's grabbing you from behind. He's coming straight at your throat with thick fingers.

And the children, with their razors, are not at all slowed down by the closed window.

You crumble under the weight of their multi-pronged attack. Something knocks you unconscious.

When you wake, you're bound to a bed by an iron collar around your throat and the dead weight of your limbs. You can barely move. The mother of the house cackles as the father holds up a hacksaw. "It's time," he says, "to feed the young ones."

He begins working on your arm. You barely feel it, as a result of whatever anesthetic he's applied. You don't want to watch, either, but you're unable to resist. Despite the literal hack job he does on your limb, he bandages your stump nicely, and does his best to minimize the bleeding so he'll be able to take each of your limbs as necessary.

It's not the most pleasant death.

You chose poorly.

At first, the room is swallowed entirely in darkness, and you cannot see its edges, its walls or ceiling, even the floor beneath your feet. Somehow, not a single shred of light follows you into the room.

As the door falls shut behind you, the room's sole occupant turns on a lamp.

Your partner, your lover, lost since the moment your car died on the side of the road, sits there, all smiles and tired eyes. "I'm so glad you're here," your partner says. "I've had the strangest dreams."

"I bet." You envelop your partner in a biggest, strongest, tightest hug, and smother their mouth with kisses.

A spiral staircase descends from the room. Together, you follow it down two flights to the ground level, and from there right out the door. Nobody stops you, nobody bars your path. The rain outside is refreshing. Together, you race to the car, stopped on the side of the road, and it starts right up for you as though it had never died.

You and your lover drive away from the spooky old house on the hill. The storm is coming to an end, and the first red line of dawn touches the eastern horizon.

Congratulations. You chose well.

It's so easy to keep the music going. The key, cold before, now seems to be a part of your hand, though of course it's not. It only seems that way. You force yourself to put it down. You struggle against your own instincts. You succeed, and drop the key on the table, where its weight leaves a crater in the rot.

Even as you put down the key, a person arrives, then more, men and women and children coming from someplace incomprehensible, all dressed in immaculate white robes that have somehow escaped the wet of the storm and the rot of the cellar. They're chanting, or humming, or in some way you can't quite grasp adding depth to the dying melody.

They close in around you, preventing you from going back the way you came, stopping you from going forward. One of the children takes your hand and whispers, "Everything will be okay."

But of course everything won't. While the music plays out to its end, they can barely see you. When the music stops, their crimson eyes and sharpened teeth and claw-like fingernails will rend you apart.

Still, they've got you surrounded and trapped, and the music box ticks out its last solitary note. There's no weight, no depth, no resonance, and the white-clad arrivals all turn toward you simultaneously. Like a note from a legitimate musical instrument, though, they fade away, all of them, their teeth the last thing visible, and even the child holding your hand dissipates, and you're free to go forward.

Go to Page 89.

"I can't do that," you say, backing away.

"What?" She's shocked. "You said you would help."

"It's all a little bit...too convenient," you say, edging toward the next door out of the library. "You had that concoction already ready before I got here. Why?"

"I've been working on this for a while," she says. "I know what I'm doing."

You shake your head.

Go to Page 189.

You open the left door and step through a swirl of darkness into what appears to be a jungle. You're pushing through a frond like a curtain. It's dark, and the storm rages, and for a moment you believe you've just walked out of the house.

But you haven't *just* walked out of the house. It is a jungle, a distant jungle, maybe a mystical jungle. A face forms in the darkness. You try to go back, but the door is closed or entirely gone.

You cannot outrun the tiger. You cannot climb as well as the tiger. You cannot fight it with your bare hands. It's easily seven hundred pounds. It stares at you, and stares, until your slightest twitch is enough to make it pounce.

You chose poorly.

You sit in one of the pews, because already your strength is failing. It's not a slow poison, per se, but it's not as quick as you might have expected. When it reaches your lungs, really only a minute or two later, you manage one final breath. You feel the blood boiling in your veins. Your heart fails next.

You die seated before this strange altar, where the author writes the final three words of your story.

You chose poorly.

"Prepared?" you ask. "No, I'm not prepared. What would I be prepared for?"

This agitates the people of the room. They talk amongst themselves, a half dozen separate conversations all at once, words whispered beyond your ability to comprehend, but finally one of them says to you, "It doesn't matter. Look into the mirror."

And there is a mirror, there on the back wall, through which a figure emerges. It's neither male nor female but something else entirely, with molten limbs and fiery eyes set too widely on its head. The mirror shatters as it steps through. It takes a deep breath of the stale air inside the house, then says something unintelligible, something inhuman—some obscene declaration that scratches the edges of reality. The walls bleed at the sound.

Flee while no one is paying you any attention. Go to Page 193.

Keep perfectly still and hope no one notices you. Go to Page 205.

The office contains a big mahogany desk with an open ledger on top of it, a wall of shelves filled with books and ledgers and journals and knickknacks—little globes, a magnifying glass, candles, figurines from different parts of the world. The figurines include ballerinas and bears and angels and knights.

The angels have all been painted black, and not by an expert.

The open ledger seems to be about household expenses, items like *Good Fellowship, Incidentals, Cigars*, and *Opera House*, as well as *Rec. of* various initials every week. The last entry appears to be from decades ago.

"Hello?" you call, but no one answered your knock and you don't expect anyone to answer your call. Briefly, in a flash of lightning, it almost appears as though someone sits in the old chair, but it's a trick of the light. There's no one there. You're alone.

Turning back toward the foyer, you notice two portraits, one on either side of the doorway, one of a woman and one a girl. They're old, faded, and tough to see in the flickering of the candles. The eyes are lifelike, and maintain the last semblance of life these portraits ever had.

You also notice a small, half door leading to a space under the stairs in the foyer.

If you wish to return to the foyer, go to Page 63.

To try the half door, go to Page 215.

You stumble back into the previous room, which had been empty before but is now filled with a variety of little demonic things, creatures resembling humanity's most twisted, distorted versions of themselves. Some sit on the shelves, some hang from the ceiling, and a great number of them cover the floor. They cause you to trip before you're really aware of them, but they don't let you hit the ground. They catch you, a dozen or more eight-inch tall demons. They're laughing and catcalling and placing bets and drinking booze and smoking all sorts of smokeables.

They pass you around like you're crowed surfing. They flip you over so you're facing the ceiling—but instead of a ceiling there's a vast portal of whirling red gases and sulfuric fumes that essentially looks like the gaping mouth of a giant worm from hell.

The demon from the other room follows you in, looks up, and says, "I see you've been saving this dance for somebody else."

"One!" the little demons call out, tossing you a foot into the air and catching you again. "Two!" This time, it's five feet, halfway to the portal, and the demon is shaking his head and laughing. "Three!" Despite all your attempts to twist and redirect yourself, they launch you into the portal, through the interdimensional tear in the fabric of the cellar, and into a hellish realm filled with burning sands and burning winds and burning laughter.

Something moves toward you, some sort of demon comprised of sand and smoke and fire, with eyes the size of your head and teeth, so many teeth. It says, "Let's dance."

It's not a pleasant dance. When it grabs you with its hundred hands, like your body becomes its marionette. Every point of contact hurts. Resistance hurts more. Soon, the *dance*, can be called that, is only pain, and you slowly realize this is how you'll spend the rest of forever, burning here under an enormous sun, burning every time your dance partner touches you, burning from now till the end of time and maybe beyond.

You chose poorly.

You go through the right door into a small dining room. The table sits eight, and eight sit at the table. There are an assortment of vegetables and sauces scattered on the table. The two youngest in the room, children no more than ten, hold their knives and forks vertically beside their plates. One of the others stands and bows when you enter. Another asks, "What's for supper?"

"You," one of the women at the table says, looking right at you. "You came from the kitchen. What's for eating?"

You look around the room, all those salivating faces turned in your direction, and give them what seems to be the best possible response: "Meat."

"Yay!" the two children say, banging their silver on the table.

"Excellent choice," one of the others says.

"What kind of meat? Mincemeat? Sweetmeats?" It's a trick question, you know that immediately, but you don't really have an answer.

"Maybe sweetbreads," one of the others says.

"Livers and eyeballs," one of the children says.

They seem completely content to discuss the possibilities among themselves, so you want to move forward, but they're not about to let you.

"Fresh meat," one of the men says, stabbing you with a long-pronged fork.

It's probably not a fatal wound, but it's only the first. Everyone at the table participates, prodding different parts of you with their cutlery, chattering amongst themselves about their favorite tastes—the tongue, one says, or the heart—which causes arguments, even as they're already sampling your fingers.

You chose poorly.

You ascend the stairs. They creak under every step. The darkness somehow thickens. At the top of the stairs is a door, a regular normal everyday door like any that might lead out of a basement in any house anywhere in the world.

But as you attempt to open the door, the stairs crack underfoot. The first crack shakes you, and you pause only a moment. With the second crack, the stairs collapse, and you plummet into a pit far deeper than the stairs ever were. You bounce off the sides of the walls, as it's a tight fall, and you crash onto a pile of wood and shattered bones. Your leg breaks loudly and painfully in the landing.

The bones will be the last company you keep.

Every attempt to climb is met with frustration, pain, and failure. When you eventually call for help, scream for help, pray for help, your cries go unanswered. There may be spiders, there may be ghosts, but the only thing you know for certain is there are dry, dusty bones, and death is slow in coming.

But death comes.

You chose poorly.

You go for the stairs. They're closer than the secret panel.

You don't even get one step before her arms have you, and her hair lashes out at you, hissing vipers with needle fangs that dig into your flesh and inject venoms. You never even see her, except for a brief flash of the green skin of her arms as she throws you backwards, over her and over the railing, and sends you down to dolls. They cheer. You're mostly dead before you hit the floor. The candles are gone, their little fires extinguished, but still you see the shapes of the dolls swarming over you like sharks, and you see the glow of her eyes looking down at you.

You chose poorly.

Down the stairs, you enter a room centered by a grand piano. Someone sits there tickling the keys, just drawing out random notes, not any kind of song. Their back is to you.

The rest of the room is filled with couches and chairs, nothing fancy, nothing worthy of a queen. Some of the seats are occupied, but all eyes are on the pianist. All light in this room is provided by a five armed candelabra on a credenza to the pianist's right, almost straight ahead of you.

No one seems to be moving, not a tilt of their heads or a twitch of their fingers, except the pianist. The notes seem almost random.

Introduce yourself. Go to Page 92.

Continue without a word into the next room. Go to Page 201.

"I'm sorry," you tell the woman you can't see on the bed, "I'm not Rebecca."

"Is Rebecca coming?"

"I don't know," you tell her. "I don't know Rebecca."

"Rebecca didn't send you?"

You approach the bed slowly as you talk, but you don't want to get too close. "No, she didn't."

"Did you bring me something to eat?"

No food, go to Page 99.

If you have food, go to Page 171.

"Absolutely, I'll help," you say. "There are a hundred or more down there."

"Three hundred nineteen, that I've counted," she says, setting the book on one of the tables and flipping through the pages until she finds what she wants. The words may be in your language, but the script is elegant and narrow and tall, so much so that it might as well be written in something else.

"It's old," she says, "so the language is rough, but...here it is." She's found something. She points. She says, "We need blood, two drops, from two willing participants." She finds a letter opener among the items on the desk. "And we need the herb mixture I've already collected." There's a small bowl full of herbs at the edge of the desk, which she grabs and brings forward. "If I've got everything right, we just need to add blood and, er, say the magic words."

Let her take a drop of your blood. Go to Page 77.

Don't. Go to Page 138.

"I didn't mean to come here," you tell her. "I got lost in a cellar."

"A cellar, eh?" She looks beyond you, back the way you came from, into the deep and deepening swamp, over cypress trees and around swarms of mosquitos and through shafts of moonlight—though you still hear the distant thunderstorm you'd left behind. "I believe you, I do," she says. "Magic flows through this swamp like blood through a vein." She lifts your hand and shows you, in her other, a firefly the size of your thumb.

"Pretty, ain't she?" the swamp witch asks. "Never mind her name, but she's one of the wisps, and she'll guide you back, if that's what you're wanting."

The wisp zips out of the swamp witch's hand, circles you three or four times, then rushes across the water to the safety of drier land. The rest of the swamp, at least for the moment, appears to be frozen in time, and a series of alligator backs offer temporary stepping stones.

To not use the alligators, go to Page 61.

To use the alligators, go to Page 248.

You turn your back on the woman on the raft. The swamp, you know, is a treacherous place, filled with dangers beyond imagining. She's probably a Swamp Witch trying to lure you to a bad end.

You retrace your steps until the bark on the cypresses gives way to something more solid, more like sheetrock or drywall or plaster or plywood, albeit covered with lichen and mucus and mold, you've returned to the cellar.

You might not be in the same place you left the cellar. You're not sure. It was all dark, dank corridors. The swampy ground has been replaced, and the sounds of the storm—still distant, yes—are no longer a world away.

There are stairs, presumably up to the house. If you'd prefer to ascend, go to Page 90.

To continue deeper into the cellar, go to Page 123.

You go through the left door into a sitting room. Chairs and couches fill the room. Candles burn on the surface of every side table. A variety of people sit throughout the room, though not every seat is occupied. Some of them look at you when you enter. Others pointedly do not.

"There's been a breach," one of the women tells you.

"A breach?"

"The portal is open. The demon emerges."

Everyone in the room repeats those last three words: "The demon emerges."

"Are you prepared?" one of the men asks.

If you don't think you are, go to Page 141.

If you think you're prepared, go to Page 188.

"I know that one," you say. "I've heard it before. The Mad Hatter."

"The *Hatter*," the man says. "Yes, yes, then what's the answer?"

"There isn't any," you say. "Not in the book."

"Maybe no," the man says. "Maybe so. Okay, then, I'll give it to you. You're right, or as right as you can be, so I'll give you a secret and a direction, and with a little luck you'll find whom you seek." He closes both hands into fists. "The word is *raven*."

"The word?"

He nods toward the door to your left. "And your best bet is that way."

He shuts his mouth and shuts his eyes and refuses to say another word.

To go through the right door, go to Page 144.

To go through the left door, go to Page 152.

"Poet," you say, throwing back the absinthe like a champion.

The bartender smiles. "I'm the madman."

"Are you really?"

"Who else would ask that question?"

You admit you don't know. "I'm looking for..."

"Oh, I know what you're looking for," the bartender/madman says. "A dream. A vision. The most perfect person ever constructed in the image of angels. I understand, I do."

"And do you know where..."

"Was here a minute ago, I'm sure," the bartender/madman says, shaking his head. "Tell me a poem."

If you have a poem ready, go to Page 120.

If you don't, go to Page 181.

The wisp wants to lead you deeper into the swamp, where the trees are unnatural, the moonlight is fading, the faint echoes of a distant thunderstorm tease you with a return to the cellar.

But you let the wisp go, and you set off back the way you know you came—you're certain of it, and you're convinced the wisp would lead you to a bad end. So you work your way through the swamp, back toward the cellar. The bark on the cypress trees becomes more solid, more like sheetrock or drywall or plaster or plywood, albeit covered with lichen and mucus and mold.

You hear the swamp witch laughing somewhere behind you. Or is it ahead of you? Quite suddenly, you're disoriented, as the walls are receding and the swamp reasserting itself, and there, on the lake just ahead of you, where you should be seeing the cellar by now, is the swamp witch's raft on the water.

She's surrounded by alligators like an army of dragons. She scowls at you. "Wisps," she says, "are generally untrustworthy, it's true, but for you to refuse my assistance—I am *truly* offended."

You turn to flee, back the way you came, but it's the lake again, and the swamp witch again, and her legion of alligators.

But none of the creatures move. Instead, the swamp witch recites words of a vaguely Caribbean nature and twists her gnarled fingers in unnatural ways. A creature of green swamp muck, maybe a man but maybe twice the size of a man, maybe larger than that, rises.

You turn to flee, but every time you turn you're facing the swamp creature again. As it moves, lifting its heavy arms, the witch laughs. Cackles even.

You back away. The creature grabs you from behind.

It doesn't have a mouth, not like a person or a bear. Instead, it absorbs you into its rich, swampy skin. It's not a quick process, though no feat of strength could free you from its hold. The green creeps over you, squeezing like a python, tightening, drawing you into itself, until you're part of the swamp creature and then part of the swamp.

The north door opens into a small room stuffed with oversized furniture, like a doll house with all the wrong pieces. Primary colors fill the room—the walls are painted blue, the couch is bright red, the chairs yellow like canaries. It all looks new and shiny, almost plastic. Somehow, three additional doors are squeezed into the room.

On the red door, black letters on a blue sign say, "Madman." To go through this door, go to Page 124.

The yellow sign on the blue door has a symbol that looks almost like a question mark with legs. To go through this door, go to Page 136.

On the yellow door, there's a red sign with black letters that say, "King." To go through this door, go to Page 170.

You don't answer. You're not Rebecca, and you don't know any Rebecca, and since the woman hidden behind the curtain on the bed is clearly not your partner, you go on to the next room.

Even as you leave, she says, "Goodnight, then."

You never see her behind the curtain, which may be a good thing. Through her room, you enter another chamber, a massive room with couches, a fireplace and mantle, and a number of books.

To explore the room, go to Page 113.

To continue on to the next room, go to Page 223.

"I'm looking for my partner," you tell her. "My lover. Lost since the car died outside the house."

"That's terrible," the woman says. "That's exactly what happened to me."

"Where's your lover now?"

She smiles sadly and looks away. "Dancing."

She descends the ladders and comes to you, puts a hand on your shoulder, and says, "This *house*, if it even is a house, has consumed them."

For a moment, you're not capable of constructing a coherent response. Finally, you ask, "What can we do?"

"Actually," she says, "I have an idea. Do you trust me?"

You don't even know. She doesn't wait for an answer. "We have to take the house down." You must be giving her a confused look, because she adds, "We can burn it down. With fire. Every timber, every beam, every panel, every room."

If that sounds like a good idea, go to Page 176.

If that seems extreme to you, go to Page 185.

The outline was clearly a violin. It seems to be the only instrument missing in the entire room. You can hear—or imagine you hear—the faint sound of a violin drifting from elsewhere in the house.

"It was a Stradivarius," a woman's voice says. She sounds sad. Melancholy, even. You turn, and she sits—she shimmers—at the harp, and drapes against it as though all the weight of the world has pressed her forward.

"It was a Stradivarius," she says again. "The only thing in this room, in this whole house, of any real value, and its voice was beautiful."

She's not real. She's an image imposed over the room. Any weight is an illusion. You ask, "Did you play it?"

"Oh, no, I wasn't the musician. That was my mother."

"Where is she now?"

"Probably hunting," the woman says. She shudders, and also shimmers, as though the distaste of what she's just said is enough to shake her right out of the world. "You better not have taken the violin, or she'll use your intestines to string it when she finds it." She shudders again, and this time fades entirely away.

You can return to the foyer. Go to Page 73

Or examine the harp, go to Page 214.

You work your way back through the dolls, all of which seem to have turned their gazes to watch you. At once, all the instruments in the music room erupt into a cacophonic symphony, the violins screaming and the piano striking a dozen keys again and again, the horns blasting, but as you step back into the room there's no sign of movement, not even vibrations on the strings of the harp, and no one in the room.

You can return to the foyer. If so, go to Page 63.

You can explore the missing instrument on the wall. If so, go to Page 159.

"I doubt that's appropriate," you tell her.

She looks you over. She even nods, almost imperceptibly, as though admiring your response. "Pity," she says. "I prefer my food to be devout."

Before you can react to the word *food*, she slashes your neck with her fingernails. The spray of blood is surprising. You see it before you feel it, but you do feel it, and you don't feel much else until she's pressing her lips to your throat and swallowing your blood in massive gulps. The pain is unbearable. When the spurting slows with your heartbeat, she sucks at your neck like it's some kind of Crazy Straw, drawing every ounce from your veins. You're dead before she's done.

You chose poorly.

The skeleton clearly belonged to a child, and the bones are definitely deformed, misshapen, bulging where they shouldn't be, and even if you're not an expert on anatomy, you're fairly certain there are extra bones where there shouldn't be.

Your examination is interrupted by whatever had been under the stairs—a corpse or a ghoul crawling from death itself. It opens its mouth, and keeps opening it, opens it until it's as big as a window, until the mouth is bigger than the thing itself, and it swallows you.

Inside its mouth, inside its belly, a ghoulish acid bath slowly dissolves your skin. It hurts, and it hurts for a long time. In the darkness within the ghoul, you hear whisperings and screaming and laughter, you see the movement of wings and the skittering of spiders and the thrusting of swords.

When the acid breaks through your skin, it works on your muscles and your bones, and eventually the pain subsides with consciousness, and you're spared the agonizing end.

You chose poorly.

You're not equipped to take on an alligator of any size, especially not a monster like this, so you run the only direction it leaves you: toward the raft.

Two steps is all you get before you find the ground it not level. You plunge into an underwater hole. The swampy water grabs you and drags you under. Vines in the muck tug at your legs and arms. You've lost your stick, and you can't break the surface to take a breath. You hear splashing, but it's probably not the alligator—it's probably just you.

Your next breath is actually a lungful of swamp, neither tasty nor rich in oxygen. You can't see, but you feel the big alligator's jaws closing on you, and you hear or imagine the woman on the raft singing as you can't decide whether to drown first or be eaten.

Either way, the bog takes and keeps you, and you never reemerge from its waters.

You chose poorly.

There's no reason to believe anyone's been in the house in ages. Despite that the door opened freely, there were no footsteps in the dust, no proof of recent habitation, no indication your partner came in this way.

You return to the deluge of the storm, to the lightning and thunder and rain, and you stare a moment at your car, corpselike on the side of the road. You see something you hadn't seen before: a church.

It's of the same kind of structure and material as the house, and looks no less promising. But it seems a more likely destination for your partner than a dark house in the middle of nowhere — admittedly, the church is also dark and in the middle of nowhere, but that's semantics.

You can abandon your partner, friend, and lover, and leave the car and the house. Go to Page 5.

You can explore the church. Go to Page 9.

You can return to the front seat of your dead car as the red rain pummels its roof. Go to Page 10.

"Your highness," you say. "I'm merely a traveler, early for the dance, and I was asked if I wished to meet the guest of honor." It's not really a lie, but you exclude everything important.

The Queen nods. "And now you've met me," she says. "You are here to dance, are you? Would you dance with your Queen?"

If yes, go to Page 122.
If no, go to Page 169.

You know you can't go back—mirror portals seem likely to be one way things, and you'll end up face to face with the valet's machete, and you don't want that. So you run. You feign right, run left, get past the valet and back to the stairs—the mirror version of those stairs. The door's open. Without the bartender, there's nothing blocking your way, and you take the steps two or three at a time until you reach the bottom.

You're on the inside of the bar, but it's not the secret side so it's easy to find the release that causes the door to swing open.

You step out and find yourself in the ballroom, an identical ballroom, behind the bar and behind the bartender, who's presently serving martinis to two of the guests.

There are a hundred guests at least, and an orchestra, and at first no one seems to notice your entrance—no one but the bartender.

"What are you doing here?" he asks in a whisper, triggering whatever secret lever closes the door. "That's my escape route."

"Why would you need to escape?"

That's when you realize the martinis were not made with gin or vermouth, and those aren't olives in those glasses. They're eyeballs.

The guests are all dead, in varying degrees of decay.

Run through the ballroom to the hall you originally came through. Go to Page 104.

Before anyone notices you, try to convince the bartender to let you go back through the secret stairs. Go to Page 183.

Try to get to the stairs on the other side of the ballroom. Go to Page 195.

Maybe it's your shoes, or the surface of the rooftop, or just the heavy rainfall. Maybe it's an edge of panic. Whatever it is, you take off at a run and your second step slips right out from under you. You crash hard on your knee, slam your forearms against the solid tiles, and slide down the side of the roof.

You crash into another flat section, but so heavily you go right through it. A moment later, you're tumbling through the air, off the edge of the roof and down the side of the house.

It's only three stories. You might survive if you don't crash headfirst into something.

You land flat on your back. Bones crack. Pain erupts throughout your body. The children's faces peer over the edge of the rooftop. You're not dead, not yet, but you're not sure you can regain your feet or your breath any time soon.

The children are there waiting for you, unhurt by their own falls. They can't be more than eight years old each, but they're also timeless, ancient, as though they'd been this age for centuries. They're swift with those razors, and they carve your life and soul from your flesh.

You chose poorly.

The room is a library with maybe five thousand volumes, an assortment of chairs and sofas, a couple of big tables and a globe. You slam the door shut behind you, and you take a moment to look around. The bookshelves line the whole wall, and stretch up twice as high as a regular room. On a ladder, in an evening gown not inappropriate for the dance downstairs, a woman looks down at you and holds some ancient, dusty tome she's just withdrawn from the shelf.

Unlike the zombies, she has living color in her cheeks, the red on her lips is lipstick rather than blood, and there's a genuine spark in her eyes. She says, "Can I help you?"

Tell her about the danger posed by the zombies. Go to Page 76.

Tell her you're looking for your lost lover. Go to Page 158.

"I'm not much of a dancer," you tell the Queen. "I appreciate your time, but I probably should be going now."

"Of course," the Queen says, nodding. "It's only right. Victor will see you to the door, won't you?"

The valet says, "Of course." He indicates the door you'd entered through.

Just as you reach the door, the Queen says, "Oh, one more thing."

You pause. "Yes?"

"I wish you hadn't lied to me."

That's when the valet—Victor—uses a machete he got from who knows where. With one stroke, he releases your head from your body.

You chose poorly.

Walking through the yellow door with the red sign that says "King", you pass through a small hall into a tiny bedroom. It's the kind of bedroom that might be squeezed into the corner of an attic, which is exactly what it is.

On the bed, there's a scepter, the kind often wielded by kings, a crystal rod with a royal emblem on the top. Otherwise, the room appears empty. When you touch the scepter, it feels *right*. It belongs in your hands. It gives you powers of vision and wisdom. It whispers secrets of the universe, secrets of time and space, secrets of alternative dimensions. You learn the fate of your partner and lover, which was horrid, or will be horrid, because you're no longer able to differentiate between now and then, past and future. You see your own corpse, still sitting on the bed, still listening to all the secrets.

Thunder cracks outside. Time cracks with it. The house cracks with it. The planet cracks. Time stretches infinitely forward. The sun explodes, and its remnants are swallowed by a celestial scavenger, the gravity of which you cannot ignore.

Time and space fall into the orbit of the celestial scavenger. It's so massive, you cannot see the whole of it at any one time, cannot even make out its dimensions. The secrets of the universe plummet into the scavenger's orbit ahead of you, so you lose the knowledge of what you're witnessing, and you lose your thread to the past—or the present. You're stretched thin as the black holes at the scavenger's heart consume you.

You chose poorly.

"Sure, I've got something," you say, fishing through your pockets for a granola bar or chocolate or whatever you happen to be carrying.

"That," she says, "is not what I want."

She explodes from behind the curtain, leaping from the bed and through the air and onto you before you can react. Her fingernails are claws, her teeth like needles, her hair a mess of living shadows, each burying its fangs into you as you fall.

You crash on the floor, the woman on top of you flailing and screaming, ripping your flesh with four arms, doing real damage real fast.

Rebecca, whoever she may be, does not come to your rescue.

You chose poorly.

There's another door out of the library, so you leave and enter another room, an antechamber of some sort, merely a room between rooms and no bigger than a walk-in closet. Beyond, there's another room, a bedroom, with a giant four-poster bed. Curtains hide the bed itself, but the rest of the room is filled with dressers and desks, so many that it seems crowded, though objectively it is not a small room.

A window looks out into the woods. The thunderstorm outside continues to rage. You cannot see the road or your dead car from here.

Behind the curtains on the bed, someone moves. She approaches the edge of the curtains but doesn't stick her head through. She says, "Rebecca, is that you?"

Answer her. Go to Page 148.

Don't answer and continue forward. Go to Page 157.

Maybe he hasn't seen you. You step, quietly and quickly as possible, to the side of the window so you're not silhouetted by the outside. The big man is shaking his head.

An old woman with wild hair and wilder eyes steps out of the shadows. "Didn't even stop to say hi, he didn't." She turns to look straight at you. So does the man.

"Please stop," the man on the bed says, his voice so quiet is cuts the room like a razor blade.

The man advances on you with long, thick strides. His fists are like sledges, his eyes burning with anger. "This is *my* family," he says.

You're no match, physically, so you try to dodge past him and make a run for it. You get past the man, only to run straight into the old woman. You go down together. She shrieks, "Get off me!"

The man lifts you by the nape of your neck with a crushing hand. You try to fight, but you might have better luck against a mountain. "Make an example of you, I'll have to."

Whatever he's planning to do, you don't make it there. He snaps your neck from behind. You hear him curse his misfortune before you die.

You chose poorly.

It's pointless, and dangerous, to run, so you drop into a defensive stance and wait for the children to approach. When they're not more than ten feet from you, one goes up and one goes down the slope of the roof. They're as sure-footed as mountain goats, even in the rain, and quick like the lightning. In this way, they flank you, and they come in from both sides with razors raised like samurai swords.

You evade the initial attack. By sheer size and strength, you manage to knock the boy off his feet. He slides down the roof and off the edge. His sister watches, horrified, screaming his name—which is swallowed by the thunder.

Then she flies at you like a berserker, all rage and fury and razors.

The blades bite, and draw blood, but down she goes, too, off the roof.

Briefly, you catch your breath. You're cut and scraped and scratched, but they're generally superficial. Rainwater drips redly off you, but you're still alive.

A sudden flurry of lightning suggests this might not remain the case if you don't get off this roof.

Worse, in the lightning you see movement—not of the human kind. One of the gargoyles is stretching its stone arms and turning its stone head in your direction.

Another flurry of lightning explodes around it, as though the statue is drawing the electricity straight from the storm.

Then it breaks free of its moorings.

Flee back toward the attic window. Go to Page 167.

Stand your ground. Go to Page 222.

"I'm something else entirely," you say, throwing back the absinthe like a champion.

The bartender grins. "I'm the madman."

"So the sign said."

The bartender/madman tilts his head and give you a quizzical look. "And you took a drink from me," he says. "Maybe I'm not the madman here."

You look down at the empty absinthe glass. Jade vapors rise from the glass, each individual strand forming a miniature ghostlike apparition. They look at you as they rise and make with the boo-shaped lips before dissipating.

The bartender, watching the same vapors, nods his head. "Hallucinations," he says. "It's the first sign."

"First sign of what?"

"Madness, of course." The bartender grins. "I don't mind. I could use a friend. Bartenders, we live the loneliest lives, you know."

You don't know if that's true, but it's hard to argue. Your tongue swells inside your mouth.

"I mean," the bartender says, removing the glass and wiping the bar top, "it would've been nice to have a friend." He winks. The poison, however, works through you, burning your veins, even as your tongue stops up your throat and chokes you.

You try to cough your own tongue out of your throat, but you're suffocating.

"Oh, I can help with that," the bartender/madman says. But he means to help with a machete from under the bar. He uses it to open up your throat. You might breathe better— maybe you do, you're not sure—but the blade cuts deep and your own bubbling blood pours down your windpipe.

It is not the most comfortable of deaths.

You chose poorly.

"How do you suggest we do that?" you ask.

"Gas. If we can get to one of the kitchens," she says. She's leaving right through the door you entered by.

"Wait," you say, but you follow her onto the landing. Down the stairs, a pack of zombies have gathered like wolves. They're falling apart, half rotten, and they stink something awful. They look up at you with vacant hunger.

"That," she says, "looks like a bad idea."

The zombies clamor over each other to reach you, shambling sloppily up the stairs.

Run down the hall. Go to Page 79.

Run back into the library. Go to Page 101.

Try to get past them and through the ballroom. Go to Page 192.

"Your highness," you say. "I'm merely a traveler, early for the dance, and I was asked if I wished to meet the guest of honor." It's not really a lie, but you exclude everything important.

The Queen nods. "And now you've met me," she says. "You are here to dance, are you? Would you dance with your Queen?"

If yes, go to Page 69.
If no, go to Page 218.

You refuse to let Shirley face the zombies alone. You're two steps behind her as she descends the stairs. It seems like all the zombies of the ballroom have gathered at the bottom of the stairs, and they're making their way slowly up.

Shirley reads the spell. The words crack as she says them. She repeats the lines over and over again as she steps into the fray.

She turns to look at you. She smiles. She says, "This is the only way." She lets the zombies take her.

At first, it seems like nothing happens except the zombies have a feast. They bite her and tear her flesh, and there's nothing you can do to stop it. Eventually, you see a golden glow, and the zombies that have tasted her flesh fall aside, stagger, crumble.

Two or three of them fall apart like statues made of ash. Two simply fall and don't move again. Some of the moaning turns into cries of agony. At least one gets a few steps up the stairs, looking at you with human eyes again, and sobs as they purge whatever black ooze occupies their stomach.

Shirley, seemingly dead for a moment, or near to death, opens her eyes again and looks at you. Her eyes, almost human, are coated with a golden film. "This," she says, "is not what I expected."

You have half a moment to respond, but it's not enough time. She says, "I'm so *hungry.*"

She launches up the stairs, an inhuman leap through the air, over the bodies of dying zombies, and crashes into you before you can flee. You fall onto your back at the top of the landing, Shirley on top of you in a fever. She buries her teeth in your chest, ripping through clothes and flesh alike.

She's a zombie, but very unlike the ones dying at the edge of the ballroom. It's a long, painful death for you, but when it's over, when it's done, you open your eyes again, an entirely different kind of zombie enthralled to your master. You're conscious enough of what you're doing, but you're just along for the ride, a witness to Shirley's long but inevitable overtaking of the entire world.

You chose poorly.

The room is a library with maybe five thousand volumes, an assortment of chairs and sofas, a couple of big tables and a globe. You slam the door shut behind you, then take a moment to look around. The bookshelves line the whole wall, and stretch up twice as high as a regular room. On a ladder, in an evening gown not inappropriate for the dance downstairs, a woman looks down at you and holds some ancient, dusty tome she's just withdrawn from the shelf.

Unlike the zombies, she has living color in her cheeks, the red on her lips is lipstick rather than blood, and there's a genuine spark in her eyes. She says, "Can I help you?"

"I'm looking for my partner," you tell her. "My lover. Lost since the car died outside the house."

"That's terrible," the woman says. "That's exactly what happened to me."

"Where's your lover now?"

She smiles sadly and looks away. "Dancing." She descends the ladders and comes to you, puts a hand on your shoulder, and says, "This *house*, if it even is a house, has consumed them."

For a moment, you're not capable of constructing a coherent response. Finally, you ask, "What can we do?"

"Actually," she says, "I have an idea. Do you trust me?"

You don't even know. She doesn't wait for an answer. "We have to take the house down." You must be giving her a confused look, because she adds, "We can burn it down. With fire. Every timber, every beam, every panel, every room."

If that sounds like a good idea, go to Page 176.

If that seems extreme to you, go to Page 185.

"I can't just recite a poem off the top of my head," you tell the bartender/madman.

"Oh, that's too bad. I'm particularly fond of love poetry because it gets in your head and mixes everything up." He shrugs. "I knew a poem once. It starts, *The world is a shadow of death*. Or is it *Death is a shadow of the world?* I forget. Sometimes, I'm easily confused." He pours another glass of absinthe, prepares another cube of sugar.

A green snake curls out of the glass. It's a small snake, smaller than a garden snake, but it grows as it slithers up and out. It swallows the sugar cube, then looks at you and asks, in an Eastern European tongue you shouldn't be able to understand, "Who's mad now?"

The hallucinatory snake strikes. The bartender/madman grins and begins to wipe down the bar. "Anyway," he says, as the snake's venom or the poison of the absinthe or both work quickly to boil your blood, "I'm always pleased to meet a poetic soul."

A fairy sits perched on his shoulder. She's green, like the absinthe, and beautiful, though tiny. She's shaking her head, and smiling for you, and she's the last thing you see before your tainted blood dissipates and oxygen fails to reach your vital organs.

You die with the hallucination of a snake clinging to your chest.

You chose poorly.

You tell the bartender, "Nothing, thanks."

He frowns at this. For a moment, it looks like that'll be the end of it, and he's returning to drying his freshly cleaned glasses, but he looks up and says, "That's rather rude, you know, barging into a bar like that and telling the barkeep you don't require his services. It's not like there's anyone else here to require my skills." He shakes his head briefly. "Makes a man feel useless, is what it does."

"I didn't mean..."

"Doesn't matter what you did or didn't mean," the bartender says. "The damage is done."

"Damage?"

The bartender puts down his cloth, reaches under the bar, and comes back up with a shotgun pointed in your general direction. "I'm just trying to earn a living," the bartender says, lifting the weapon and aiming it right at the center of you.

Stand and fight, go to Page 32.

Run back the way you came, go to Page 96.

Run forward, down the next hall and toward the stairs, go to Page 129.

"Let me go back," you say, pleading, but the bartender's shaking his head.

"It's too late," he tells you. "You reek of life."

It's true. You've been alive all your life. You can't help but reek of it. The guests for the dance have started to notice. The orchestra has noticed. One by one, the instruments are losing the thread of their melody. As they do so, the dancers are losing their step.

The dead couple who'd just received their bloody martinis have their vacant eyes on you. Chipped teeth show as they grin. Someone else, somewhere not too distant, says, "Brains."

Maybe, maybe not.

The dead dancers close in on the bar, all of them now, three and four thick, in too many numbers to escape. That doesn't stop the bartender; while you're distracted, he's slipped away. The secret door closes behind him, leaving you trapped in the zombie-filled dance hall.

Trapped, and at the center of attention.

They close in, and though you attempt to defend yourself—you shatter three good bottles of bourbon trying to fight—it's pointless. They overwhelm you, and then they're pulling at you, and someone comments, with a slur, on the delicacies offered by the hosts.

You, of course, are the delicacy. They tear you apart.

You chose poorly.

The panel will clearly slide away, but there's no obvious lever. Even moving the photograph triggers nothing. You check the instruments on the wall beside it, looking for something to open the door. You lift violins and try to move levers that are merely pegs.

You can leave the music room and return to the foyer. Go to Page 73.

You can return to the missing instrument. Go to Page 159.

Maybe pushing the harp back in place will open the door. Go to Page 276.

To apply brute force to the secret door, go to Page 270.

"That seems a little extreme, don't you think?" you say.

"I've been here a hundred years," she tells you. She's definitely not a hundred years old. At least, she doesn't look it. Maybe the house does lie.

"Good luck with that," you say.

She nods. "Of course. I understand. Go, do what you think you need to do."

There's another door out of the library, so you leave and enter another room, an antechamber of some sort, merely a room between rooms and no bigger than a walk-in closet. Beyond, there's another room, a bedroom, with a giant four-poster bed. Curtains hide the bed itself, but the rest of the room is filled with dressers and desks, so many that it seems crowded, though objectively it is not a small room.

A window looks out into the woods. The thunderstorm outside continues to rage. You cannot see the road or your dead car from here.

Behind the curtains on the bed, someone moves. She approaches the edge of the curtains but doesn't peek her head through. She says, "Rebecca, is that you?"

Answer her. Go to Page 148.

Don't answer and continue forward. Go to Page 157.

"I came here," you tell her, holding yourself steady, "looking for my partner. Do you know anything?"

"Partner?" The swamp witch crinkles her eyes and stares into your soul. "Tell me more."

You tell the witch everything—almost everything—from your dying car and the useless mobile phone to your missing lover and the spooky house on the hill—though you leave out sneaking in through the cellar door. As you tell your story, she listens intently.

Finally, she says, "Your story moves me." She nods once, then again, as though considering something in her head. "I intended to feed you to the swamp, but I once believed in something very much like love, so I'll send you back."

She snaps her fingers, and a green twinkling light—a firefly, maybe?—whizzes through the cypresses, right past your ear, to hover in front of her sounding very much like a hummingbird. "This is a wisp," she says, "which are generally unreliable, but this one—forget her name, it doesn't matter to you—she'll guide you true."

The wisp takes off, passing the other side of your head. When you turn to see where it's gone to, it's bouncing around about twenty yards deep into the swamp. You tell her thanks. Turning away and nearly mumbling, the swamp witch says, "Go, before I change my mind."

The wisp zips forward twenty and thirty feet at a time. You have to move quickly to keep up, though the swamp does everything it can to slow you down. The roots of trees try to trip you, the limbs grab at you from above, a swarm of mosquitos dive bomb you as you move. The trees are giving way to cellar walls again, until they're not, and the wisp may be leading you somewhere but you can't be sure where.

Continue following the wisp, go to Page 108.

Try to get back on your own. Go to Page 155.

You shake your head. "The final dance," you tell her, "belongs to my lover."

The woman frowns. It's the last frown you'll ever see. "That's cruel, to deny me a final dance."

The hungry horde tear the two of you apart violently and messily.

You chose poorly.

With every confidence, you say, "I am."

"Excellent."

The people in the room all rise and lead you toward the center of the room. A mirror dominates the back wall. In its surface, you see a swirling darkness, a maelstrom of cloud and smoke. A figure steps forward.

"Closer," someone says at your ear.

But you don't move. Getting closer to the mirror seems rather inadvisable.

The figure in the mirror speaks directly to you, so that you don't hear its voice with your ears. "Do you know the word?"

"The word?" you say. But you know it, of course, because the man in the other room gave it to you. "*Raven.*"

The figure in the mirror rages. It screams and throws blasts of fire in a dozen different directions. The flames smash the inside of the mirror. It melts from the inside. Reflective sludge pours onto the floor. You step back to keep out of its molten pool. In the newly formed image, you see only the ceiling tiles of this room. The figure, whatever it was, is gone.

The occupants of the room have all either fled or vanished, leaving you alone. There's another door, further down on the same wall as the one you'd entered through. It's ajar. There's not much choice but to go through it.

On the other side, there are two doors, and a man so elderly his flesh drips in melted leather He narrows his eyes are you. He says, "There was a prophecy."

"Was there?"

"You were foreseen," he says. "Now you must choose. Your lover or the tiger." He makes no other move and says nothing else. The doors on either side of him are identical.

Press him for more information. Go to Page 121.

Choose the left door. Go to Page 139.

Choose the right door. Go to Page 247.

You say, "I'm sorry, I can't."

Frowning, she says, "I understand. Go, do what you need to do. Just don't go downstairs."

There's another door out of the library, so you leave and enter another room, an antechamber of some sort, merely a room between rooms and no bigger than a walk-in closet. Beyond, there's another room, a bedroom, with a giant four-poster bed. Curtains hide the bed itself, but the rest of the room is filled with dressers and desks, so many that it seems crowded, though objectively it is not a small room.

A window looks out into the woods. The thunderstorm outside continues to rage. You cannot see the road or your dead car from here.

Behind the curtains on the bed, someone moves. She approaches the edge of the curtains but doesn't peek her head through. She says, "Rebecca, is that you?"

Answer her. Go to Page 148.

Don't answer and continue forward. Go to Page 157.

The spider women taste you intermittently. You're unable to resist, unable to move, unable to escape. They keep you for a while, days if not weeks, while your strength and sanity wane, and eventually your life.

You chose poorly.

You retreat back into the ballroom, toward the bartender and his shotgun. Seeing you, he lowers the weapon, and says, "This is rather a surprise."

"Zombies," you say.

He rolls his eyes and raises the weapon. "Again?" he asks. "Damn things won't stay down."

When they reach the hall doorway, they stumble over each other trying to push their way through. The bartender lets loose another shot, which shatters one of their heads.

"Quick," he says. "The stairs."

Go to Page 129.

Look at how slowly those things move. "We can get around them," you say.

The woman follows you down the stairs. She believes you. You spoke with such confidence, such surety, such authority. But it's a long way through the ballroom, and a hundred zombies or more swarm around you from all sides. The bartender, behind the bar, shakes his head and looks away. That path is cut off, but so is the hallway that enters the ballroom. More zombies are arriving from that direction.

In the middle of the ballroom, you and the woman stop. You're surrounded, thoroughly and completely, and there's no place to run.

"Well," the woman says. "Can I have a final dance?"

If yes, go to Page 119.
If no, go to Page 187.

You go back for the door you came through. The knob burns your hand when you grab it. The creature of smoke and fire says something else in its inhuman tongue. Your ears split at the sound. The door in front of you pulsates. Waves of heat surround you from all directions.

The creature grabs you by the back of your neck and lifts you into the air. Its hand seems insubstantial, all smoke and vapors, but its grip is like hot iron. It's not content to simply lift you, either. It crushes your throat from behind, squeezing until the vertebrae crack and crumble and your head comes free of your body.

You chose poorly.

With every confidence, you say, "I am."

"Excellent."

The people in the room all rise and lead you toward the center of the room. A mirror dominates the back wall. In its surface, you see a swirling darkness, a maelstrom of cloud and smoke. A figure steps forward.

"Closer," someone says at your ear.

But you don't move. Getting closer to the mirror seems rather inadvisable.

The figure in the mirror speaks directly to you, so that you don't hear its voice with your ears. "Do you know the word?"

"The word," you say, but you don't know the word so you guess. You make several guesses. Good, educated guesses, the kind that might work in other circumstances.

The figure laughs and reaches out from the mirror to take your hand. With that brief contact, it switches bodies. Your body, possessed now of an ancient demonic spirit, laughs and turns away from the mirror and speaks to its disciples. You hear none of it. The mirror fades. The walls are fire. Brimstone. The sulfuric fumes burn your throat and lungs. And the torturers, the infinite torturers, drag you deeper into this fiery realm to punish you for all your sins, real and imagined, and all the sins of the world, real and imagined, and all the sins ever committed by man or god.

You chose poorly.

You race for the stairs, trying desperately to not look like you're racing, but you stink of life—no doubt because you've been alive since you were born—and the dead who dance are beginning to notice your stench.

You're beginning to notice theirs.

You reach the stairs. You climb the stairs. Behind you, there's moaning, and the orchestra continues to play its minor key waltz, but some of the zombie guests shamble toward you.

The stairs are wide, carpeted, and lead to a landing which allows you to go either left or right.

To the right, there's a hall, and maybe you can put some distance between yourself and the zombies' slow pursuit. Go to Page 72.

To the left, there's a doorway, and maybe closing the door will give you some protection. Go to Page 168.

"Excellent," the man says. "I'm terrible at riddles, myself, so I hope you can answer this one. *Why is a raven like a writing desk?*"

If you recognize the riddle, go to Page 153.
If you do not, go to Page 210.

"You want me to let a spider woman bite me so her venom can infect my blood and we can use it to control the zombies?" you ask, not certain you follow everything the woman says.

She nods. "Precisely."

"Okay, then."

She opens the second door—the library has only the two, and you hadn't even noticed the second because it was hidden behind shelves—and you pass through an antechamber of some sort, merely a room between rooms no bigger than a walk-in closet. Beyond, there's another room, a bedroom, with a giant four-poster bed. Curtains hide the bed itself, but the rest of the room is filled with dressers and desks, so many that it seems crowded, though objectively it is not a small room.

A window looks out into the woods. The thunderstorm outside continues to rage. You cannot see the road or your dead car from here.

Behind the curtains on the bed, someone moves. She approaches the edge of the curtains but doesn't peek her head through. She says, "Rebecca, is that you?"

"We need your help," you tell the spider woman.

She peeks out from behind the curtains. "My help?"

"With the zombies."

She hisses. "What do you need?"

"Venom."

"That," she says, "I have plenty of."

She skitters forward, four arms and four legs propelling her toward you too quickly. She crawls right to you, drags herself up the front of you with her four arms, looks up at your face and says, "There's no value in the dead. I need fresh food."

"Of course you do," you tell her, doing everything you can to hold your ground.

She bites your arm, then backs away, halfway to the bed. "There," she says. "That should be enough to kill you, but not too quickly."

"Um...thanks."

You go back the way you came. The woman in the library has mixed everything else together, and has used a needle to prick her finger. She's dripping her own blood into the concoction.

"Did she bite you?"

"Yes."

"Quickly, then," she says, "before the venom makes you unable."

Already, your limbs are going numb, and they move like dead weights at the end of long strings. But you manage to reach the woman. You hold out your hand. She jabs your finger but you don't even feel it. Blood drips into the mixture she's making.

"I hope that's enough," she says.

"Now what?" you ask. Your voice is slurred. This might have been a mistake.

"Now," she says, looking at the other door—the zombies are busting it open, cracking and splintering it. There's really no time left. "Now, I consume it." She tips the bowl into her mouth and swallows the strange mixture. She makes a horrified face. "It's terrible."

The zombies break through the door.

She stares at them. She trembles visibly. She says, "You will obey me."

In response, the moaning goes mostly quietly. One of the zombies not yet through the door says, "Brains?" It's definitely a question.

"Sure, yes, here," the woman says, gesturing toward you. "He can't resist any more anyway, and the venom's going to kill him." She smiles at you. "Thank you, by the way. Your sacrifice saved my life."

Your limbs are basically nonresponsive as the zombies fall all over each other to reach you. With the paralysis, you're also numb, so while you watch them tear your flesh apart, at least you don't feel it. Not really.

You chose poorly.

You hesitate, then stand aside so the author can return to work. You ask, "Will it end happily ever after?"

"It might have," the author tells you, "but it'd be a lie. There's always a sequel."

You know the story in the book is the story of this old spooky house—specifically, the story of the old spooky house as it is this very moment. "Will I find my partner?"

The author is already writing. "Stories," he says, "are an act of discovery. But I'm sorry to say, your partner is lost to you forever. At least in this life."

You refuse to accept such an ending. You say, "No."

The author looks at the empty chalice. "You've already drunk the poison."

It's true, and you know it. The wine is working its way through your system, dissolving and shutting down your internal organs.

Accept your fate, go to Page 140.

Beg for help, go to Page 208.

You go through the right door and into a small dining room. The table sits eight, and eight sit at the table. There are an assortment of vegetables and sauces scattered on the table. The two youngest in the room, children no more than ten, hold their knives and forks vertically beside their plates. One of the others stands and bows when you enter. Another asks, "What's for supper?"

"You," one of the women at the table says, looking right at you. "You came from the kitchen. What's for eating?"

You look around the room, all those salivating faces turned in your direction, and give them what seems to be the best possible response: "Meat."

"Yay!" the two children say, banging their silver on the table.

"Excellent choice," one of the others says.

"What kind of meat? Mincemeat? Sweetmeats?" It's a trick question, you know that immediately, but you don't really have an answer.

"Maybe sweetbreads," one of the others says.

"Livers and eyeballs," one of the children says.

They seem completely content to discuss the possibilities among themselves, so you want to move forward, but they're not about to let you.

"Fresh meat," one of the men says, stabbing you with a long-pronged fork.

It's probably not a fatal wound, but it's only the first. Everyone at the table participates, prodding different parts of you with their cutlery, chattering amongst themselves about their favorite tastes—the tongue, one says, or the heart—which causes arguments, even as they're already sampling your fingers.

You chose poorly.

You walk past the pianist, not interrupting the music, and enter a dining room, a dining *hall*, capable of seating twenty or more. At least that many people are milling around doing pretty much nothing—until you enter, giving them someplace to focus their attention.

It takes only a few seconds to realize they're all dead, each face more decrepit than the last as they turn their attention to you. They moan and groan and grunt as they advance toward you.

There's no way forward. There's no way back, either, because the music room zombies, which you had walked right past without even realizing it, have gathered around the doorway and are pushing through. One mumbles, "Brains."

You fight with whatever you can get your hands on. A candlestick. A knife. An exquisite piece of silverware that might all by itself be worth more than your home.

But the zombies feel no pain. They close in, grunting and shuffling, their hands impossibly strong, their teeth impossibly sharp.

You chose poorly.

You move quickly. The zombies are slow, just like all the old movies suggest, so you're able to run straight into the next room before any of them can get their hands on you. Or their teeth.

Unfortunately, there are more in the next room. It's a dining room, a dining *hall*, capable of seating twenty or more, and at least that many zombies are milling around doing pretty much nothing—until you rush in, giving them someplace to focus their attention.

There's no way forward. There's no way back, either, because the music room zombies have gathered around the doorway and continue to advance.

You fight with whatever you can get your hands on. A candlestick. A knife. An exquisite piece of silverware that might all by itself be worth more than your home.

But the zombies feel no pain. They close in, grunting and shuffling, their hands impossibly strong, their teeth impossibly sharp.

You chose poorly.

You laugh. You scoff. You refuse to pay, and you climb out of the bar. You feel as though you've escaped something, though you're not quite sure what. You return to the storm, the relentless rain and the thunder and the wet, but the barkeep grabs your shoulder and yanks you back into the bar.

"You," she says, "are being rude." Her eyes have an amber glow you hadn't noticed before, and her grip on your shoulder is more than strong, it's crushing.

You start to apologize, and even offer to pay, but you can't get the words out. She's pulverizing the bones in your shoulder, and she's taken your hand in her other and crushes those, as well. Though you resist, or attempt to resist, her strength is supernatural, and she makes dust of as many bones as she's able before you pass out from the pain.

You're lucky, in a way. You won't wake up again to find all your bones reduced to powder. You simply won't wake up at all.

You chose poorly.

You stare at the drink a moment, then look up at the bartender and say, "The sign outside the door says *madman.*"

"Right you are," the bartender says.

"So thank you, but no." You push the glass back toward him.

The bartender shrugs. "That's fine," he says. "This stuff's been known to cause hallucinations. You'd have to be mad to welcome those." He lifts the glass and throws back the absinthe like a champion, slams the glass back down to the bar. "Hits the spot, it does."

"I'm looking for someone," you tell him.

"Yeah, I know, we all know, you ain't exactly subtle," the bartender says. "Hey, watch this." He forces a breath from his mouth. It emerges as a wisp of green smoke. "You like that? It's not real. I'm hallucinating it."

If he's hallucinating it, how can you see it?

He does it again. The smoke lingers, and briefly takes on the shape of a green fairy.

He does it again, this time spouting a tiny flame. "Ah, now that's what I'm talking about," the bartender/madman says, tendrils of green leaking from his lips.

The door behind you won't open again. You can't back any further away from the bartender than you already are. His grins at you, takes a deep breath, and shoots a stream of emerald flames at you.

The hallucinatory fire burns you up completely.

You chose poorly.

You don't move. You don't dare draw attention to yourself. The people of the room also remain perfectly still. They had waited, and your arrival somehow triggered this, and now the creature—the demon—is free.

It continues speaking, its voice an agonizing noise. The creature reaches for one of the people and touches her face. It smokes and smolders. When it removes its smoky hand, it has left a mark, three fingers and a thumb, on her face.

It touches a second person, burning its brand into his face, as well.

It reaches for you, and you're unable to flee. It grabs your face but it knows, somehow, that you're not like the others. It's not enough to brand you, it burns through the flesh and into your skull until the bones melts and it can close its fist over a chunk of your brain matter.

It's a painful end, and it lasts far longer than it should.

You chose poorly.

The door opens easily and reveals a set of stairs descending a short distance to another room, stone all around, with marble markers on the walls indicating the names of archbishops, deacons, celebrities, whoever else might be interred under this cathedral. Some of the names are distinctly Eastern European or Spanish or Arabic. One of the marble markers has been removed, but the vault appears empty. That marker is not the only one without a name engraved into it.

To explore the crypt in more detail, go to Page 280.

Another set of stairs descends even further. To take them, go to Page 364.

It's an old book, dry leather that creaks when you touch it. The pages are thin, the writing in it ornate, the illustrations immaculate. But at first, you can make no sense of it. The letters themselves are unlike anything you're familiar with. Certainly, they say something, but there's nothing you can recognize. The beasts in the illustrations are nonsensical, amalgamations of animals you know—spiders with the heads of queens, lions with eagle's claws, snakes with wings.

All at once, the wine gives you vision, and you can read the book.

You flip through the pages. There's stories of Spider Queens and the dead dancing and mushrooms from the outer reaches of the galaxy. There's a story about the Swamp Witch on her raft in this very cellar, and you see yourself in the story, going to the Swamp Witch and telling her your quest.

You turn the page to discover what happens next, but the page is blank.

"Ah," someone says. "I see you've uncovered my handiwork."

When you turn, there's the author himself. His accent is unique, his eyes soft, his voice breathy but deep, and he carries a fountain pen like a weapon. The nib *looks* sharp, but his eyes definitely are.

"I intended to complete that section today," the author tells you. "May I?"

If you will move aside to allow the author to continue writing, go to Page 199.

If you will not move aside, go to Page 341.

"Please," you say, "let me live."

"That would require a drastic revision," the author says, shaking his head. "Perhaps in another life," he tells you.

"Another life?" Already, your strength is failing. It's not a slow poison, per se, but it's not as quick as you might have expected.

"There are many worlds," the author tells you. The poison reaches your lungs, and you manage one final breath. You feel the blood boiling in your veins. Your heart fails next.

"It's okay," the author says. "Sometimes, life can be cyclical."

He doesn't write the final three words of your story, not while you still live. Instead, he says, return to Page 1.

You accept the offered zebra. "Thank you," you tell the boy. "And what's your name?"

But the boy isn't there anymore. Neither are the other toys, just the painted zebra in your hand. Instead of the boy, you hear the whispers. They're distant, at first, and impossible to understand, but they're persistent, and getting louder.

Your candelabra doesn't offer a lot of light to the room, but combined with the luminescence of the storm and the rapidly flashing lightning, you see the door behind you is no more or less open than before, and the door ahead remains closed.

When you step forward, one of the whispering voices says, "Don't."

When you step back toward the other door, another of the whispering voices says, "Not that way."

"Then what way?" you ask.

The whispers offer no answers.

If you want to go forward anyway, go to Page 26.

If you want to wait and listen to the whispers, go to Page 268.

If you want to go back, go to Page 273.

You think about it. You try to apply logic, and the roundabout logic of riddles, and really you cannot fathom what the answer might be. Eventually, the man is tapping the back of his knuckles against the table. "C'mon," he says. "It's not so difficult as all that, is it?"

Finally, you admit the truth: "I haven't the slightest idea."

"Ah." He nods. "That's too bad." He bangs the table again, and says, "Don't you *read*?"

"Read?"

"It's an old riddle, but it's not ancient, and it wasn't handed down to us from before recorded history," the man says. "It's from *Alice*."

It takes only a full second to realize he means *Alice's Adventures in Wonderland*.

"What's the answer, then?" you ask.

The man smiles. "I haven't the slightest idea," he says, "is as close as it gets. You're right, after all, so I'll give you a secret and a direction, and with a little luck you'll find whom you seek." He closes both hands into fists. "The word is *raven*."

"The word?"

He nods toward the door to your left. "And your best bet is that way."

He shuts his mouth and shuts his eyes and refuses to say another word.

To go through the right door, go to Page 144.

To go through the left door, go to Page 152.

As you race back for the comparative safety of the music room, all the instruments at once erupt into a cacophonic symphony, the violins screaming and the piano striking a dozen keys again and again, the horns blasting. The door slides shut just before you reach it. You almost run into it, but stop in time. All the motion, however, causes two of the candles to go out, leaving you with one tiny flame in the darkness.

Behind you, the dolls are giggling. They sound like maniacal children, twisted and evil creatures about to taste victory—but what they're really about to taste is you. The first one that clings to your leg, you're able to swat away. The second bites you with its miniature mouth. Trying to swat it away, you lose the last of the candles.

So you don't know what they use when they slash at your ankles. You don't know what they use to stab your shins.

"Don't touch," one of the bigger dolls says behind you. You imagine the big blue-eyed doll from the stairs shaking its head. They're dropping on you now from the shelves, climbing your clothes, digging into your flesh with tiny glass hands, wrapping your legs with their rag bodies, tripping you, and bringing you down.

The dolls fall on you like a swarm.

You chose poorly.

"I appreciate the help," you say.

The doctor smiles as though this is a given, but he's already done with you. He says to someone you hadn't seen yet, "Nurse, please give him the tour."

"It'll be my pleasure."

The nurse is an unrealistic caricature of a nurse, all voluptuous curves and cheap bottle blonde hair that falls in waves and covers half her face. "This is the entry room, obviously," she says. "This is where you entered."

That's not much of a description. She's guiding you gently by the arm through the room and toward a hallway. At each door, she describes what's inside. "Dissection. Vivisection. Supplies. Quarantine. Oh, in here we've got lollipops." She's opening the door. "Suckers, I think they called them. I'd like one. Would you?" She's already inside. Plastic shelves hold boxes of surgical tape, gauze, hypodermic needles, medication with long Latin names, boxes of latex gloves, long coils of rope, and a bowl full of lollipops.

The nurse has already unwrapped one and stuck it on her mouth.

If you will also take a lollipop, go to Page 35.
If you decline the lollipop, go to Page 70.

You climb out of the basement, careful on the stone steps. The stale air of the den seems blissfully cool and fresh, but only by comparison.

In the foyer, the lightning provides a brilliant show of shadows, shadows which seem almost like marionettes come to life.

To climb the stairs, go to Page 30.

If you feel like it's time to leave this house, go to Page 164.

To go through the doorway, go to Page 233.

Other than the music, which has already faded, there's little to suggest anyone had been there. The chair remains covered in dust, but the strings themselves are not, as though this isn't the only time they've played themselves. Perhaps there's a breeze from somewhere, though you felt nothing, that touches the strings.

That wouldn't explain the melody. But it was only a few notes, so maybe your mind filled in the blanks to make it sound intentional.

It's a big harp, and it looks heavy, but you notice one other peculiarity: the harp has been moved, and recently. Only an inch or two, but the proof is in the dust underneath, and the discoloration of the floor. It's slight, yes, and barely visible, but it's undeniable. The front edge of the harp has been pushed at least two inches aside.

And if you look at the wall where the harp now points, behind a faded framed photograph of an elderly woman, the wall conceals the vague outline of a door, a secret door. You might not have noticed if you hadn't examined the harp.

Try to get through the door. Go to Page 184.

Push the harp back to where it had been. Go to Page 276.

The half door has a small knob that takes some effort to move, and the hinges protest with a squeal not unlike a dying pig. You have to bend to see into the space under the stairs, and find a set of stairs descending into thick darkness. Cobwebs drape the bare walls, which are unfinished on this side and reveal the bones of the house, two by fours and the like. The steps are carved out of stone.

You lead with the candles. Once you're through the doorway, you no longer have to bend, but the descend is tricky. The steps seem solid, but in places the stone has crumbled to dust, and there's also sand or dirt making it slick under your feet. Your footsteps are relatively quiet, but every sound echoes through the chamber.

When you reach the bottom, the floor is packed dirt. Shelves on the walls hold buckets, hand-labeled cans, and an assortment of kettles, bowls, and cauldrons.

A tall but otherwise small table, like a chest on its side, dominates the center of the room. An iron key, and nothing else, rests on top of it, presumably to unlock the chains that have been attached to the stone wall.

No one thought to unlock whoever had been cuffed there. All that remains are a collection of bones. It's difficult to imagine how badly this person would have suffered, but clearly it was long ago.

In the spandrel beneath the stairs, something stirs.

Examine the table, which clearly must contain something inside. Go to Page 116.

Examine the skeleton more closely. Go to Page 162.

Check under the stairs. Go to Page 235.

Flee from whatever's moving. Go to Page 240.

Some of the books are bound in leather, some have been sewn together, and at least one is entirely encased in wax. You're careful not to damage the seal—who knows why it's been clamped shut like that.

None of the books seem to stand out as an obvious lever to open any sort of secret passageway.

From below, the dolls sound restless—or your imagination does.

There's no ladder on the iron walkway, though the books reach higher than you can, even on the tips of your toes. There are few objects on the shelves other than books—but you lift the framed photograph of a young girl, move the stone the size of your fist, and touch an onyx ball, candle holders, bowls, and vases. You search for something in any of the carvings and engravings built into the shelves, various woodland creatures, faces a la the Green Man, something that looks suspiciously like a bust of Pallas, even a Medusa with her head full of vipers.

Finally, after too long a time, you discover a lever in the ironwork railing itself, right at the top of the stairs. It triggers a panel of the bookshelves to swing inward and reveal another room.

If you want to enter the other room, go to Page 50.

If you want to go back to the wax book and break it open, go to Page 241.

You don't need to be told twice.

Also, you know there's nothing behind you that's going to help. So you go forward, straight into a room of thick, absolute darkness that swallows the lights of the candles before they can reach your eyes.

From outside, the sounds of the storm disappear entirely. There are no windows—or at least, no windows allowing any light into the room. You can see so little, it's a question of whether the room itself has swallowed all light or if your eyes have failed. Looking back, you see nothing of the room you left or the boy or the storm that had been flashing in the windows just a moment ago. You can't even see the door.

Stepping back, you cannot find the door.

All you see is darkness and all you hear is silence. You reach for one of the candles on your candelabra. You feel the small heat of its flame. You pluck the candle and drop it on the ground.

You don't hear it land.

You bend to retrieve it but cannot find it, cannot find anything, not even the floor—though clearly you're kneeling on something. Tentatively, you step forward. You find something to stand on in the darkness.

That's how you spend the rest of your days—how many days, you can't even guess—wandering in the darkness, in the silence, not even able to hear your footsteps or your heartbeat. You're not sure you're alive. You imagine things in the darkness, but they're things made of darkness. They're things made of silence.

You chose poorly.

"I'm not much of a dancer," you tell the Queen. "I appreciate your time, but I probably should be going now."

"Of course," the Queen says, nodding. "It's only right. Victor will see you to the door, won't you?"

The valet says, "Of course." He indicates the door you'd entered through.

Just as you reach the door, the Queen says, "Oh, one more thing."

You pause. "Yes?"

"I wish you hadn't lied to me."

That's when the valet—Victor—uses the machete. With one stroke, he releases your head from your body.

You chose poorly.

You step carefully through the room, over and around the dolls which cover every surface except on the stairs. As you walk, it seems like their eyes remain on you, like the eyes in paintings, so you move a little more quickly.

It's only a few steps to get to the stairs, but as you're about to climb you realize there is, in fact, one doll just a few steps up. It's child-size, maybe three feet tall, with a glazed porcelain face and large blue eyes. It stands in such a way that you couldn't see it from the secret door, but you can't simply walk around it without moving it.

So you move it.

You pick up the doll and put it down on the floor. Carefully. It feels fragile and cold. It stares at you with malevolence when you move it, but surely that's in your mind, right?

In the music room, someone runs a bow across the strings of a violin. It's discordant and angry, a slash of music cutting the darkness. When you look back, all the dolls, every doll whose face it lit by the candles, stares at you now, at the bottom of the stairs, just as they'd stared at you at the door on the other side of the room. Every doll's head has moved to follow your progress.

You also here footsteps. Tiny footsteps. As though dolls you cannot see are moving swiftly through the darkness on one side of you or the other.

Retreat to the music room, go to Page 211.

Race up the stairs, go to Page 237.

The south door opens onto a long, narrow attic room. The ceiling comes down at an angle, with alcoves carved out of it for dormer windows looking onto the woods. There's a town shrouded in darkness. There's trees, and the howling of wolves, and the distant sounds of bells when the thunder eases up momentarily.

The room is filled with crates and boxes and chairs, all coated with dust and cobwebs, all of it untouched since long before the door was replaced. The floor is carpeted, so you walk in relative silence. On an old, twin size bed, laying on a dirty mattress, is part of a person. He's still alive, but instead of limbs he has bandages. He wears an iron choker attached to a chain which holds him down to the bed.

If you want to ignore him and assume he's not really alive anyway, go to Page 126.

If you would rather approach and ask if he needs help, go to Page 225.

The table holds secrets. It takes only a few seconds to find the release that opens its hidden door. Inside, on one of three shelves, you find a book and pen. The pen is old, a quill, dry, dusty, and fragile, and it breaks in half when you touch it. The book, also, is arid, and its leather cover is cracked. There is no title. Opening it, you find pages of notes in tight, fancy cursive. The last entry says *Day 37, the subject has finally, mercifully, ceased to suffer. Forthwith, I'll have to cut open the corpse and discover what can be found inside. I hope and pray, with every ounce of my soul, it will not be so bad as I suspect.*

Previous entries say, *The raven disappeared, the raven she gave birth to just yesterday. I don't understand it, and I question my own sanity, but I know the bird did not fly free.* Another entry says, *She screams, she screams day and night, she screams with inhuman lungs. She screams as though this is my fault and I can somehow save her. I cannot. She must know this. In her heart, she must forgive me.*

The first entry says, *Day 1, Emily, aged 12, blue of eye and blonde of hair, forsaken to my care to examine and understand. My doctor friend insists she's not human. My initial examinations concur. Her heart races and her flesh is cold and her eyes turn inwards. She doesn't speak, not in any language with which I'm familiar. When I took the scalpel to her, however, her blood ran red.*

There's nothing else in the table.

To leave this small basement, go to Page 213.
To explore the skeleton, go to Page 267.

The gargoyle roars like a stone lion, a sound greater and more terrible even than the thunder. It flexes its stone claws and shows all its stone teeth. It moves with impossible speed, revealed in the staccato strobe of the lightning, and crushes your brittle bony skull with a single swipe of its stone hand.

You're dead before your body falls.

You chose poorly.

Moving on, you enter another bedroom, this one empty, its bed a four poster again but without curtains. Otherwise, it's nearly identical, but inverted, so that the bed is on the opposite wall.

As you make your way across the room, which seems vaster as you walk, you hear a voice. "Rebecca?"

The voice comes from above you, above the bed. A woman, with four legs and four arms, clings effortlessly to the ceiling. You hadn't noticed her. She looks down at you with a hundred eyes. "You're not Rebecca," she says.

"No, sorry, I'm not."

"You didn't bring me anything to eat, did you?"

"I'm sorry, no," you say. "I'm looking for someone."

"I'm hungry."

She spits at you. She spits venom. It stings your face, and blinds you, and burns your flesh. You stumble backwards, flail to protect yourself, but it's too late. She's on you almost immediately, wrapping you in her webbings. It's hard to resist. Your muscles respond sluggishly to your efforts.

She pauses after binding your legs. "Sister," she says.

The woman from the other room says, "I let him pass. It's only fair."

"Top or bottom? Or left side or right?"

"Which side has the heart?"

Your attempts at speech are muffled and muted and slow.

"I think it's the left."

"I'd love the heart side."

Rather than continue wrapping you up, they tear you in half, down the middle, so one sister can have the side of you with the heart.

You chose poorly.

Without a word, you throw back the absinthe like a champion.

The bartender watches you as you set the glass back on the bar. He smiles, but it's a weak smile. He says, "For the record, I'm the madman."

The silence stretches uncomfortably until you ask, "What makes you mad?"

"Inhumanity," the bartender says. "The inevitability of inconsequence. Mankind's failure to rise above its station." He shrugs. "Incivility."

It's quite a list.

"That poison," the bartender/madman says, "was laced with absinthe and sugar."

As if on cue, the poison begins its work on your veins, melting them like acid from the inside. Your stomach twists. The first twist is not enough to double you over, but the second cramp comes before the first is even done.

"That's it," the bartender/madman says, leaning over the edge of the bar to look down at you. "Let it all out."

You try to vomit, to purge the poison from your system, but another wave of stomach cramps drops you to your knees.

"That's not the way to do it," the bartender/madman says. "You're just letting it run rampant inside you."

You are, but there's nothing you can do about it. Vital organs are shutting down. Your heart has stopped beating. Your lungs have stopped pulling breath. Even your skin aches at the end.

You chose poorly.

You don't get too close. "Are you okay?" you ask. "Do you need help?"

His eyes snap open. "Help," he says. He moans it, really. His eyes are unfocused. They swim a bit before finding you. His mouth keeps moving, but there's no force behind the words so they don't reach you.

You lean closer.

"Help," he says again. "It's too late for that. Look at me. Look what they've done."

He flails the stumps that are his arms and legs.

"It's too late for me," he says, "and it's too late for you."

He bounces up, biting at you, gnashing teeth that have been filed sharp. You avoid his mouth. It's not hard.

But as you back away, you back into the arms of someone — or something — else. They wrap around your chest. You struggle against them. The voice, this one much deeper, whispers in your ear. "You're a fine one."

The words are pure malice. You flail, you fight to break free, the effort eliciting laughter from the limbless man in the bed and from others in the room, a woman, and maybe two or three children.

The man who has you puts a cloth to your face. It's chloroform, or something similar, and it takes no time for your consciousness to fade.

When you wake, you're bound to a bed by an iron collar around your throat and the dead weight of your limbs. You can barely move. The mother of the house cackles as the father holds up a hacksaw. "It's time," he says, "to feed the young ones."

He begins working on your arm. You barely feel it, as a result of whatever anesthetic he's applied. You don't want to watch, either. But you're unable to resist. Despite the literal hack job he does on your limb, he bandages your stump nicely, and does his best to minimize the bleeding, so he'll be able to take each of your limbs as necessary.

It's not the most pleasant death.

You chose poorly.

Choose Your Doom

"I won't stay long," you tell the spectral girl, "but my friend is lost."

"I had a friend once," the girl says, thrusting the doll in her hands toward you. It's one of the more life-like faces, a child's face, frozen in a mask of terror. You sense the weight of a soul within those glass eyes.

"What happened to your friend?" you asked.

She lowers the doll and shakes her head. "I died, and she disappeared."

"I'm so sorry," you say.

"Will you be my friend?"

Say yes, go to Page 239.

Say you can't, go to Page 244.

There's no point wasting time in a room full of fresh, fetid corpses. There's no sign of your partner and lover anywhere in here, thankfully, and there's no other direction.

When you try to get through the door, however, the dagger won't come with you. It refuses to move beyond the threshold, it holds your hand on the inside of the room even as the crater, left by the collapsing demon, grows.

When you release the dagger, it drops into the crater and buries itself, pointed edge down, in the body of something crawling up from the darkness.

Through one room, through another, you make your way back toward the cellar entrance. The music you'd left behind continues to grow.

You can turn and go down the center corridor. Go to Page 40.

Or you can follow that sound to the passage that had been on your left. Go to Page 65.

You step away, but don't run. When you don't immediately answer, he blinks again - over empty sockets—hops to his feet, and says, "Cat got your tongue?"

A cat on the other side of the room hisses.

The corpse hisses back at the cat. For a moment, they stare at each other, then the corpse—face it, the thing's been possessed by a demon—lurches forward for the cat. It races away, and at the last moment the demon grabs you by the scruff of your shirt and brings your face close to his. His stale breath is beyond decayed. He asks, "Do you know the twist?"

With inhuman strength, he lifts you off the ground and twists your body around entirely, and entirely again, until it rips in the middle. Then he drops both halves of you into the pits of an inferno, laughing the whole time.

You chose poorly.

You pick up the ring. It's cold in your hands, shockingly cold, much more so than you would have imagined. It's too small to fit on your finger, but you look at it more closely and you test it over your finger anyway, not really expecting it to push past your fingernail.

It slides right over your knuckles and, improbably, fits perfectly.

You examine it on your finger. You almost feel as if you've just been engaged. You can see who wore it before: a young woman, barely more than a girl, her hair in fingerwaves, her lips curved in a genuine but not overly generous smile.

You almost see her before you *actually* see her. She's on the other side of the table, holding out her hand, looking down at the ring on her finger—on her finger and yours simultaneously, as if both hands share the same place.

When you try to move away, you're unable to. She slides around the table, stepping into your body and raising the ring to look more closely at it. She says something about it being lovely, something about Roger, something about the handcuff on her finger.

You've got no control of your own body anymore, if it even is your body. It's the ring, and the woman with the ring. Then she says, "Let's blow this popsicle stand."

Since you cannot do anything else, you accompany her through a series of rooms to a hallway, down a set of stairs, and into another world, where it's still the Roaring '20s and everything is jake. There's dancing in the ballroom, flappers, bobs, plenty of giggle water, and the more the woman inside you takes control, the less you see and the less you feel. Your own senses are fading, and you're falling backwards into your own mind—into the darkness in your mind, into a form of oblivion.

You chose poorly.

You waste no time retreating to the room with all the statues. The door slams shut of its own accord. Thunder rattles the house. Something skitters in the gloomy shadows. The chandelier fizzles and flickers.

One of the statues falls at you.

You manage to get out of the way, but it's close, closer than you would prefer. There's no one there to have pushed it, but certainly all of the statues are bottom heavy, their marble plinths a part of the sculpture. It did not fall on its own.

Another statue tumbles toward you.

And another.

It's an effort, to stay out of the way, and you drop the candelabra as you evade the statues. They're coming at you, guiding you in a particular direction, toward an open window you hadn't noticed.

The next falling statue catches your arm, and it's almost enough to knock you to the floor. It's heavy, and it'll probably bruise, and it tears through your clothes and scratches your flesh.

You're at the window now, as far from both doors as you can possibly be, and another statue is slowly tilting in your direction.

Try to get out of the way but stay in the room, go to Page 100.

Try to get out of the way by going out the window, go to Page 290.

Leaning closer to the mirror, you begin to see what might be your own face reflected in its dark surface. Bringing the candelabra closer doesn't change what you see. Eventually, your face resolves itself—not in any detail, so you appear no more distinct than an underdeveloped Polaroid.

You lean closer, trying to catch some hint of detail, or figure out why it won't show you anything. It's almost a compulsion now, so you lean still closer, almost close enough to touch the mirror, which is definitely glass but wrong somehow. Warped. Disturbed.

When you try to pull away, you lean further in instead, and find yourself slipping into the mirror. Your flesh moves through the cracked surface rather easily, but the candelabra resists. It hits the glass and shatters a chunk of it and tumbles out of your hand on the outside of the mirror.

Leaving you inside the image staring out at a room where the tiny flames of the candles have touched the carpets and started to grow.

The bed takes quickly to the flames, which also climb the walls with an impossible rapidity. Behind you, a girl says, "Don't worry. You're not alone."

But you are alone. Alone in darkness, alone in a shadowy realm with no direction and no substance, nothing but a mirror looking in on a burning bedroom. There's a man there, someone you don't know, searching frantically for someone, a child perhaps, before the conflagration consumes everything. He looks desperate. Angry. When he looks into the mirror, he sees you, and he picks up the candelabra. The mirror is only partly broken. You see through the rest of it, and in the corner you see the confused bits being reflected by the shards.

The man yells something. It's like watching a silent movie. He swings the candelabra and shatters the entire mirror. The image goes dark, and vanishes entirely, leaving only the darkness from within the mirror. And the girl's voice saying, once again, "Don't worry. You're not alone."

She says it at irregular intervals. She never says anything else. You wander and search and sometimes see images that might be the other sides of mirrors elsewhere in the house or even elsewhere in the world, but you never really see anything at all.

You chose poorly.

Through the door, you enter a claustrophobic music room. Here, the room is dominated by a grand piano under a thick coating of dust. Violins and trumpets are mounted on the walls, alongside horns you don't quite recognize, and bizarre stringed instruments. A cello stands next to one of the many chairs. A harp sits in the corner.

What catches your attention is the blank spot on the wall. It's visible because of a discoloration shaped vaguely like a violin. The dust, heavy everywhere else, is disturbed here.

The strings of the harp are plucked in a brief melody. When you turn, no one sits there, but the sound echoes briefly and the strings still vibrate.

Or is it a trick of the flickering candlelight?

Turn your attention back to the missing instrument. Go to Page 159.

Examine the harp. Go to Page 214.

You walk into the next room, where a massive bed looks to be made with layers of silky cobwebs. Once upon a time, a girl slept there and died there, a young girl, possibly Anna. You're sure of it. You can almost see echoes of the event, and it's heartbreaking.

There's a large mirror and a bureau and a writing desk. There's an assortment of combs and brushes in front of the mirror, as well as an unlabeled pill bottle. The pills it contains have dissolved together and warped into some sort of miscolored piece of abstract art. It's horrifying to look at, as though the once—white pills have been marbled with lemon flakes and viridian. At some point, someone had been taking those pills; the bottle is only half full, or half empty.

The mirror reflects only darkness. Even the candles don't seem to be break its surface.

To examine the mirror more closely, go to Page 231.

To explore the room more thoroughly, go to Page 281.

To go through the next door, go to Page 285.

Moving closer, the flickering candles reveal nothing but a nest of rats, their black eyes glimmering yellow in the light, their whiskers twitching. There are babies, and the mother rat stands defiantly upright between you and her young.

There's nothing else visible under the stairs except the weight of decades and even centuries. The house is old, yes, but its foundations are older still. Maybe there's always been something on the top of this hill.

Examine the table. Go to Page 221.

Examine the skeleton. Go to Page 267.

You stare up at the body—the body still alive—but do not run. The ghost, again, in the bed, looks at you with wide eyes. She shakes her head and pulls the covers up so she can hide underneath. The voice of the skeleton underneath says, "Hide with me."

The next door opens. Someone's stepping into the room. The body above screams. The figure looks at the near-corpse. He carries a heavy hammer in one hand, some kind of sword in the other.

You have time only to slide under the bed and perhaps escape its attention. The screaming, combined with the thunder that's even louder now that the door's open, masks the sounds of your movement.

Next to the skeleton, you realize you can't push past it. You're stuck there, under the one side of the bed, with no means of egress but the way you came in. And you'd slid through the fresh blood, smearing it.

The figure steps heavily into the room, into the blood, the hammer and sword hanging in his hands.

He raises the sword. The screaming stops abruptly. A second passes. Another second. Then he pulls the sword down. It shines wetly as it hits the candelabra on the floor where you'd abandoned it in your urgency to hide.

He taps the candelabra twice with the edge of the sword. He grunts. He turns one way then the other, slowly, deliberately, as though he has all the time in the world.

Then he lifts the sword and plunges it into the bed. It goes straight through the cobwebs and the ghost, if she's still there, and the mattress and the frame, and straight into your hip.

You cry out. You can't not. The pain is immense. He twists the weapon, they withdraws it, hurting just as much coming out as going in.

Then he smashes the hammer down from the side of the bed. The heavy head of that hammer catches your jaw.

You're not alive long enough to feel the next blow.

You chose poorly.

John Urbancik

You're already on the stairs, so you rush forward, up and around, as the dolls behind you cackle and rattle their glass eyes. From the music room, the faint sound of crying reaches you, and it's almost enough to make you pause.

The iron landing above the dolls circles the room, which you didn't realize until now is round, with a railing on the outside and a library of books on the inside.

The dolls clamor up the stairs after you.

You race around the landing, all its books, the iron shaking beneath you as you run. Left or right, it doesn't matter. You reach the top of the stairs again. The first of the dolls is only just reaching the top steps. It's the blue-eyed childlike doll you'd moved.

There must be an exit somewhere, another secret door hidden in the shelves, but you don't have a lot of time to find it.

The doll carries a knife.

Where did the doll find a knife like that? It's a kitchen knife, a carving knife, and you're the intended meal.

As you retreat from the advancing doll, the grated floor gives way. You plummet into darkness, losing the candelabra and all its light, and land among a sea of dolls. They swarm, crawling over you and stabbing at your face with whatever other weapons they've found, biting when they can, holding you down so when the big doll jumps from above, it lands heavily on your chest and plunges the carving knife into you again and again.

You chose poorly.

You tell the bartender you have no preference, and he expertly prepares and serves an amazingly sweet and delicious drink. "You know," he tells you, "the dance doesn't start for another hour. But the guest of honor—well, would you like to meet her?"

Yes. Go to Page 112.
No. Go to Page 125.

"Yes, of course," you tell her. "I'll be your friend."

"I'd like that," she says. The dolls, however—in your periphery, in the shadows, just outside of where you can reach—seem suddenly nervous. They're shaking their heads or maybe groaning.

The girl hands you the doll. "Here," she says. "Hold Anna for a moment."

You take the doll. She reaches behind her for another, slightly larger and of a similar design but blank, without features. She takes Anna back and gives you the blank doll. "The doll has such pretty eyes."

When you're look at the eyes, they're without color, mere glass, perhaps reflecting your own eyes in the candlelight. "It's nice," you try to say, but no sound forms, and you realize you're being held by you—or a blank version of you—and you're looking at your former self through the doll's glass eyes.

The girl snatches the doll—you—away before your body topples over. The other dolls drag the husk of you away, leaving your essence inside the doll, unable to move, unable to scream, unable to look at much of anything until the spectral girl aims you in that direction.

She swings you around a bit, and introduces you to other, similar dolls: *Anna* and *Christina* and *Lucy* and *Sue*. Over the next few hours, you're set at a miniature table for a tea party, and all the dolls are served imaginary tea, and the girl eventually says, "Oh no! Someone's poisoned the tea!"

That's when the last of your candles finally dies.

You chose poorly.

Before whatever's under the stairs can get you, you run back to the stairs and up, as quickly as you can. So quickly, the candles go out. This doesn't slow you down any until the stone beneath your foot crumbles. You drop heavily, smashing your knee on the stone, then tumble back down the stairs, smashing your head two or three times as you go. Something in your leg snaps. The pain shoots up your entire body.

Whatever had been under the stairs—a corpse or a ghoul, a thing crawling from death itself—reaches you at the bottom of the stairs. Its fingers are claws. It tears through your clothes and your flesh. Its breath is rancid and rotten, and its teeth jagged, as it consumes you.

You chose poorly.

It takes another minute to retrace your steps and find the sealed book. It appears to have been dipped in green wax, long ago, and then stamped, perhaps with a signet ring, with the image of a dragon. It might be a genuine ruby at its heart. There's also marks all over it, as though someone has scratched at it, perhaps testing its limits.

The wax completely obscures the book, its cover and spine, so there's no indication as to what may be inside.

Without ceremony, you crack open the wax. It's rather easy, actually, and corresponds with a tremendous crack of thunder outside that shakes the house to its foundations. The wax barely resists. After the first crack, the rest of the job is merely peeling away the pieces. Some stick to the leather binding—presumably leather, though it looks suspiciously like human skin. There's nothing written on the spine. The words and image on the cover have faded to mere memories.

Opening it, after a few blank pages, you find a title page. It's titled *Bestiarum Vocabulum*, in fancy, old-fashioned calligraphy that's almost indecipherable. The image is clear and distinct, a sharp ink as black as the heart of darkness: the face of a Gorgon-like beast, vipers in the hair and jagged teeth, with green ink to indicate the eyes. As you watch, the green dissipates, leaking off the page as a thin wisp of smoke.

When the ink is gone, a strange calm and silence settles over the house. The dolls in the room below rustle for a moment, then go perfectly still. Someone, somewhere in the house, screams, and it cuts the darkness and scratches at your bones.

Then a woman behind you, immediately behind you, so close you feel her breath as she exhales for the first time in countless ages and says something in so old a variation of your language, you cannot understand.

If you want to flee, go to Page 146.

If you prefer to stay and see what she might say, go to Page 275.

As you race back for the comparative safety of the music room, all the instruments at once erupt into a cacophonic symphony, the violins screaming and the piano striking a dozen keys again and again, the horns blasting. The door slides shut just before you reach it. You almost run into it, but stop in time. All the motion, however, causes two of the candles to go out, leaving you with one tiny flame in the darkness.

Behind you, the dolls are giggling. They sound like maniacal children, twisted and evil creatures about to taste victory—but what they're really about to taste is you. The first one that clings to your leg, you're able to swat away. The second bites you with its miniature mouth. Trying to swat it away, you lose the last of the candles.

So you don't know what they use when they slash at your ankles. You don't know what they use to stab your shins.

"But it's okay," the girl says. "You can stay with us forever." The dolls drop on you from the shelves, climb your clothes, dig into your flesh with tiny glass hands, and wrap your legs with their rag bodies, tripping you, and bringing you down.

The dolls fall on you like a swarm.

You chose poorly.

Climbing the stairs, you reach a landing where there are two doors. The ceiling is lower here, and a window looks out onto the woods. You see your car and a church and a road stretching into darkness. Blasts of lightning seem to run exclusively in one direction—south to north. You remember something someone said to you once, about nothing good coming from the north.

The two doors lead north or south.

There's nothing else on the landing. The wood paneling is old, and there's a miscolored rectangle indicating where a painting or photograph had previously hung.

The north door appears to be older, marred with scratch marks in the lower panels and along the edges. To go through this door, go to Page 156.

The south door looks so new, it might have been replaced only yesterday. Go to Page 220.

"I have to find my missing friend," you tell the spectral girl. You describe your partner. "Have you seen anyone?"

"Only *Anna*," she says, again showing you the doll.

"I have to find my friend," you tell the girl.

Her eyes go wide. "Or you both will die?"

"I hope not."

She frowns. She says, "It's not so bad. I have my dolls."

"That's very nice," you tell her. "You have quite a lot of them."

She shrugs. "I would have more, but I never see anyone."

"Well," you say, standing back to your full height—you had stooped a little to speak with the girl—"I better go find my friend."

"Anna wishes you luck," the girl says.

"Tell Anna I said thank you."

Go to Page 160.

You waste no time arguing. You rise to run, but it's already too late. The skeleton from under the bed grabs your ankle. Though the bones look fragile, their grip is unbreakable. The body above—the body still alive—opens its mouth and screams. The ghost, again in the bed, looks at you with wide eyes. She shakes her head and pulls the covers up so she can hide underneath.

Someone—or something—smashes the back of your head. You don't go immediately unconscious, but the pain is immense and there's a spray of blood. The bones wrapped around your ankle make it difficult to turn or move. The second strike is not a blunt object like the first but a blade, and it drives straight into your spine, between vertebras. Quite suddenly, you feel nothing below the cut. Your legs collapse beneath you.

The third blow is the blunt object again, and it shatters your skull.

You chose poorly.

You back away with your fists open and your hands down. "I don't want no trouble," you say.

"You don't get to back away from this," the old man tells you. He might be talking about more than just his fists, he might be referring to the house and your missing partner and your dead car, but it's his fists he's working with now. He swings, catches you on the jaw, and throws you backwards off the porch. Your head cracks when you hit a rock in just the wrong place. There's blood, and the old man jumps down to finish the job. He's a former boxer or something, so every punch is like a brick to the face. A quick mob forms around you, townspeople cheering on the old man, calling him Luke or Duke, something like that. No one steps in to help you or stop him or end the fight, and you never even manage to get back on your feet.

You're pummeled to death in the rain.

You chose poorly.

You open the right door and step through a swirl of darkness into what appears to be a jungle. You're pushing through a frond like a curtain. It's dark, and the storm rages, and for a moment you believe you've just walked out of the house.

But you haven't *just* walked out of the house. It is a jungle, a distant jungle, maybe a mystical jungle. A face forms in the darkness. Your partner and lover bursts out of the foliage and envelops you in a hug and whispers, "I knew you'd find me."

You try to go back, but the door is closed or entirely gone. Instead, you're merely in the woods surrounding the old spooky house, which is completely dark, a black silhouette against the stark midnight storm.

No—not midnight. It's morning, and the first weak light of dawn strains to break through the clouds. You and your partner return to the car where you left it. It starts right up. You and your lover drive away from the spooky old house on the hill.

Congratulations. You chose well.

Quickly, and with a fair amount of trepidation, you run across the backs of the alligators to the shore. The wisp doesn't wait but whizzes forward, twenty and thirty feet at a time. You have to move quickly to keep up, though the swamp does everything it can to slow you down. The roots of trees try to trip you, the limbs grab at you from above, a swarm of mosquitos dive bomb you as you move. The trees briefly give way to cellar walls again, until they thicken again, and the wisp may be leading you somewhere but you can't be sure where.

Continue following the wisp, go to Page 108.

Try to get back on your own. Go to Page 155.

The valet is only gone a minute or so before returning. He still carries the machete, as though it's part of his uniform. Indeed, his uniform is extraordinarily formal, and you're still wet from the thunderstorm. "The Queen," he says, "will receive you." Holding the door open, he gestures inside with the machete.

You step into the Queen's room.

It's enormous. You could fit entire houses in this one room. The ceiling is two or three stories high, the numerous windows just as tall, with wallpaper out of the eighteenth century, as though you've stepped into a throne room of some ancient European palace.

Marble statues adorned with gold represent all twelve gods of the Greek pantheon. The chandelier, made up of a thousand and one candles, throws flickering light everywhere, reflecting off the crystals hanging there—possibly emeralds and rubies and sapphires—casting infinite shades of color throughout the room.

The cleanest, brightest light falls on the Queen herself. She sits on one of two thrones, red velour lined with gold, equal in size and stature. The other seat is dusty, coated in cobwebs, but the rest of the room is immaculate and wonderful and overwhelming.

It's almost enough to make you forget everything.

And the Queen herself: she sits on her throne in a lake of ebon fabric, complex lacework and brocades, silver around her neck and hanging from her ears and in her fingers. She holds a scepter, wields it, really, as though it's a weapon. With it, she motions you to the center of the room, where all eyes of the court would be looking—but you're alone in this throne room with the Queen and her valet.

You step to the center of the room, and bow as best you can before her royal highness. She laughs. "Rise, child, and tell me who you are and what you want."

Lifting your head, you realize the Queen is in fact ancient—beautiful, yes, but it's not the beauty of youth that radiates from her. She's as dusty and web-filled as the empty throne beside her, her eyes the palest you've ever seen, and the silver spider hanging from a chain over her décolletage almost looks alive.

Tell her the truth. Go to Page 75.

Tell her something else. Go to Page 177.

You run.

It's not a retreat, you tell yourself, but a calculated effort to get past the obstacle—the wolf that stands like a man, the creature with claws and teeth and eyes straight out of nightmares. You go through the woods, hoping the rain will mask and mute your noise. You don't see the wolf man move, but that means nothing. You go deeper into the woods than you think you need to in an effort to get around the creature.

You don't *hear* the wolf giving chase. You look back, over your shoulder, and see no sign of it. You see nothing, really, but darkness, a deep and deepening darkness that penetrates the entirety of the woods.

It's no mere woods, not anymore. It's a forest. A jungle. And though you try to head back toward the road, you see no sign of that, either. The trees thicken. The undergrowth gets gnarly, as though the roots are rising to entangle you. Even trying to go back the way you came, you only find yourself getting deeper into what's becoming a quagmire. The ground is soft and wet. It sucks at your feet.

The tree limbs swipe at your face, and fronds heavy with rainwater cut your cheeks and arms and legs. Eventually, a vine catches your hand and holds you back. Another snares your foot and almost trips you.

Trying to disentangle yourself, you manage only to get yourself more deeply entwined. And though you're making no progress forward or back, the trees seem closer, more thickly shadowed, more threatening, until at last you're pressed against one at your back and another at your side. The limbs have you braced, and the vines have you knotted, and the bark of the trees digs into your flesh like slow, blunt knives.

A tree stands in your path so close, you can feel its breath and see its eyes. The trees crush you between them, a slow and arduous and seemingly unending process, until the pain causes you to lose consciousness, which is something of a blessing. The trees continue for a long time after until you're dead.

You chose poorly.

The bathroom is beautifully done, with marble floors and walls, towels that look softer than anything you've ever seen, a vanity large enough for a public restroom in Grand Central Station. The shower is massive, larger than your entire bathroom. Water rains down from the ceiling, steam rises and flows over the glass wall. There's a woman there, thoroughly lathered, rinsing her hair and singing. When she sees you, her eyes go wide, she throws a palm against the glass, and says, "You shouldn't be here. Look out!"

The warning is too late.

Someone—maybe the man from the wine cellar—smashes the back of your head with a blunt object. You're dazed, and you go down, crashing knees first on the hard marble floor.

The woman in the shower mouths, "The knife" just before it cuts through you. Your blood splatters the glass doors of the shower. The woman watches as you're hacked, again and again, in a reversal of sorts from the famous scene in *Psycho*. You see flashes of the knife reflected in the glass.

It's the last thing you see.

You chose poorly.

Descending the iron stairs, it takes a moment for the light of the candles to reach the dolls. They're all looking up at you, and they appear agitated. They seem to shift and tremble when you don't look directly at them. They've been harmless so far, so you suspect they'll continue to be safe, and you only need to get through the dolls to get back to the music room.

Four or five steps from the floor, you see the girl. She's in a big white dress like any girl of ten might have worn a century ago. She's got one of the dolls in her hands. She looks at you, big blue translucent eyes, so you see the dolls behind her and reflected off of her as though she's a weak mirror. She says, "You're not supposed to be here."

To continue the conversation, go to Page 226.

To push quickly through the room and back to the music room, go to Page 242.

The salt's not going to help, he's already telling you that, so instead you go for the cross-shaped dagger. It's cold in your hands. The corpse releases it and smiles at you and whispers, "Good luck."

When the demon bursts into the room, laughing so maniacally its jaw has come unhinged so it can open its mouth more widely, you meet it with the sharp end of the dagger. Briefly, the iron dagger flashes hot and the eyes of the demon go wide. He says, "Oh, so you *are* a dancer." But that's his last breath. He crumbles to dust, drops to one knee and shatters and disintegrates, leaving a crater in the floor.

A moment later, there's only darkness, the dim lightbulbs, the corpses, the dagger cold again in your hands.

Go back the way you came. Go to Page 227.

Explore the room some more. Go to Page 320.

You wake sometime later, who knows how much time, slumped against the bar, looking up at the old man and the barkeep. He's scowling. She's grinning. Spores are growing out of the pores in your chest and arms and fingers. The transformation isn't complete, but you're becoming something fungal. Mushroom thoughts already infect your brain. They permeate every bit of you. You try to move, but your muscles have either already atrophied or completely dissolved.

"You see," the old man is saying, "there's a special kind of fungus, it comes from the depths of space, from a time before this planet even existed. It feeds us, stranger, and sustains us, and thanks to people like you, we'll never run out. There's always a new crop."

"Pluck the spores," the barkeeper says.

And that's exactly what they do. They pull the spongey orange stems from your skin, and your senses move with each of them. You feel the pain of separation, but that's brief. You feel the moist soil and the soft trees, and you join a field—no, a farm—behind the town, and in time you're spread very thinly across some acres, but all sensation never fades.

Instead, you feel when parts of you are harvested, and when parts of you are mixed into their strange brew, and you sense the bits of you dissolving in the liquid and being absorbed into the bodies of the townspeople. You have no ability to move, no voice with which to speak, and the world is dull and muted, but it's never-ending, and perhaps even at the end of the planet, when the earth is destroyed, you'll continue to persist in some form, your mind trapped within the fungus.

You chose poorly.

Entering the cathedral again, now the shadows seem darker, the columns taller, and the ceilings higher. Unless your eyes deceive you, there's movement in those shadows, movement that might be merely bats but might be something more sinister.

Your feet seem unusually loud on the marble floor, even with the storm outside. Your heartbeat, too, sounds more pronounced, though it's probably only in your ears.

The stranger pulls the door shut behind you. It echoes through the cathedral.

"This way," the man says, guiding you with a firm hand at your back toward one of the many doors inside the cathedral. "We'll be dining shortly."

The person kneeling near the altar turns their head to glance in your direction, then faces forward again. Your host looks older than you originally thought, practically ancient, even dusty. Not a drop of rain seems to have touched him. Beyond the wood door, he walks you through a chapel with pews and giant stained glass windows—primarily red, they depict scenes of war and violence. The ceiling is low here, and there's another door behind the altar.

"We're so pleased you could join us," the man says, opening the door and ushering you through it. "It's rare we get guests, but tonight has been bountiful, indeed."

In this room, there's a big table, around which sit a dozen men and women in fancy dress from varying ages—coattails and canes, crinoline and corsets, eyes behind painted handheld fans. A seat at the center of the table remains empty—presumably for the old man accompanying you now. They're drinking red wine from chalices of glass and gold. Chatter dies immediately when you enter, and all eyes fall on you.

Just then, another door bangs open, and a chef arrives with the main course on a huge serving tray. He sets it on the table, taking up fully half the space, and the old man tells the chef, "We'll have another for our meal tonight, I think."

The chef looks you up and down, rubbing his hands together, and says, "Excellent."

John Urbancik

That's when you realize the meal that's been set upon the table is, in fact, your partner, tied and bound, not cooked at all. And the diners—*diner* might be the wrong word—have visible incisors.

Run. Save yourself. Go to Page 350.
Try to rescue your partner. Go to Page 358.

You push through the right door into another room, this one entirely empty except for an extraordinary rug on the floor. Windows on one side face the woods. From here, you see a graveyard and the shadowy façade of a church. Lightning sparks across the sky and the thunder is more prominent here than it had been.

From the ceiling hangs a very basic chandelier. There are no bulbs, but little bits of electricity drip like golden sparks from the empty light sockets.

Under those sparks, where there hadn't been before, a little boy plays with a zoo of wood toys on wheels—each flat piece is shaped like an animal, which was then drawn on the sides. He's rolling them an inch or two at a time in procession, a great parade of animals, but he pauses to look at you and smile.

In a flurry of lightning, the smile transforms to a look of terror, and the numerous scars on his face become visible. He squeezes his eyes shut and yells, "Go away!"

You can continue through the room to another door. Go to Page 217.

You can go back. Go to Page 230.

You can try to communicate with the boy. Go to Page 277.

You scramble back, up to your feet, and in the direction of those chisels and a heavy hammer to arm yourself. You feel a little silly, facing off against this man with such makeshift weapons. He, at least, has done nothing to threaten you.

But he faces you. He looks at the weapons in your hands, and the blood on your chest and arms and legs. He meets your eyes and says, "Children. They need constant attention, do they not?"

When you don't immediately answer, he bears his fangs and his claws, setting his own weapons against yours, and attacks.

You get at least one good swing with that hammer and maybe knock a chunk of his skull off, though not before he gouges your chest with his fingers. He touches the side of his wound. That smile looks absurd on his three-quarters of a head. You'd crushed part of it, but there's not enough blood.

"I'll admit," he says, "that hurts. But you're no match for me and my *children*."

With the word, they're at your legs again, coming from behind. You lost track of them during the melee. It doesn't take much to drop you to your knees. As they're chomping on your back, their father lunges forward with impossible speed and severs your hands at the wrists—both simultaneously—with his fingernails.

The pain, the shock, it's all too much—but it's not done yet. He grabs you by the throat and lifts you back to your feet as the children tear chunks of flesh from your thighs and calves. He looks amused, and his head is already visibly reshaping itself. He crushes your windpipe, his claws piercing your throat until they find the carotid artery. Before you can bleed out, he crushes the life out of you.

You chose poorly.

"Maybe I'm the ghost," you tell the man sitting there. When he moves his arm, it goes transparent for a moment, as if its solidity has to catch up. When he stands, his whole body shimmers. His eyes sparkle in the light of the candles on your candelabra. Although he seems to push the chair back from the table, it doesn't actually move.

He rests his pipe on a piece of wood designed for it. As he approaches you, the pipe and its holder vanishes. He looks up and down the length of you, not in any obscene way but with all the awe of a scientist or a child. "I can't say I recognize your style of dress," he says. "Must be the opium. Absolutely amazing." He looks you into the eye, points at you with his pipe—which you thought you saw him put down—and says, "You've got to be the most amazing hallucination I've ever seen. Not like that ape. Not like the princess. You've got substance, and depth, and detail. And your style of dress—I've never seen anything like it. Well, just that one time."

"What one time?" you ask.

He shakes his head. "I know how to handle hallucinations. Heroin."

"I'm not a hallucination," you tell him.

He goes to one of the shelves, where a variety of bottles contain pills, powders, and liquids. "Heroin cures everything," he says. "Or is that aspirin?" He turns to you. "Have you got a suggestion? No, don't answer that. A hallucination would never tell me what to take to banish it back to—back to wherever you come from."

A sound catches his attention—a sound you both hear—and you both turn to the doorway where the sound originated. You don't see anything or anyone, but he obviously does. He says, "Anna, what's wrong?" Apparently, she responds. He nods gravely. "Yes, of course. I'll bring the heroin and the laudanum, I'll give you whatever will help best."

You don't see Anna, or anyone else, and looking back to where the man had been standing, you no longer see him or pill bottles, either.

But the door is still there. To go through it, go to Page 234.

To explore the game room more, go to Page 346.

You don't answer, and the old man continues. "I'll tell you what you want," he says. "You want sanctuary and solace. You want safety from the fingers of the forest. But I can tell you, there ain't none of that to be found. Not here."

He rises so quickly you barely see him move. He's in your face. His skin is like cracked leather left too many years in the sun. His eyes are all pupil in the dark of night. His breath is stale and sour and wet with the storm. He's got his fists up. "If you ain't a coward, give me your best shot."

If you ain't a coward, give him your best shot and go to Page 46.

If you are a coward, stand down and go to Page 246.

You continue down the hall for what seems like forever. Finally, the hall ends in a ballroom. A *Phantom of the Opera* chandelier hangs in the middle of this room. And though the house was big from the outside, it seems like the room is as big as the house. There's a long bar along one side, with shelves full of bourbon and scotch and tequila. A bartender wipes clean one of the wine glasses, looking at you the whole time. When you finally see him, the bartender smiles, puts down the glass, and says, "What shall I get you?"

Be specific. Tell him what you want to drink. Go to Page 33.

Ask for whatever's good. Go to Page 238.

Refuse the drink. Go to Page 182.

You bend to one knee and slowly, almost tenderly, lift the edge of the covers to peer under the bed. Darkness, first, but as your eyes adjust you see a child's skeleton clinging to the bottom of the bed frame—not merely clinging, the bones are supported by frayed and moldy rope.

The skull faces you. Teeth are missing. The jaw moves, ever so slightly, or moves in the shadows of your flickering candlelight. A boy's voice whispers, "Please don't tell."

You whisper back, "I won't."

But the skeleton cannot possibly be the source of fresh blood. Still kneeling, you turn your attention to the ceiling. That body is fresh. The blood has stopped pouring but still drips from the fingers and the wound—the wound in the chest, a massive gaping hole, still wet. It hangs from the ceiling by ropes tied around its wrists, its ankles, and its belly. The eye sockets look toward you—there are no eyes, not anymore. The head shakes. The lipless mouth says, "Run."

Or don't. Go to Page 236.

Run to Page 245.

The door on the right opens onto a small bedroom. There's a crib with a mobile, all thin wooden circus animals and clowns and a ringmaster.

It's hard to tell in the flickering candlelight, but there's a stain on the blanket inside the crib. It's a white blanket, so the stain stands out. It's brown now, but it might very well have been blood. You can't be certain. It's not a recent stain.

On the wood floor, there's another bloodspot.

The window blinds burst open, banging around outside hard enough to crack the glass. The storm is growing violent.

In the reflection of the glass, even with that big crack cutting through the edge of it, you see a woman standing over the crib, standing and looking down. She looks up and her tear-glistened eyes lock on yours.

When you turn, the room is empty. No woman stands over the crib.

On the dresser, there are an assortment of pill bottles and spoons and a crumpled handkerchief that's gone completely red. It wasn't originally red.

There's nothing else in this room, and certainly no sign of your missing partner. You hurry out. To go downstairs and into the office, go to Page 142.

If you think it's a better idea to go downstairs and leave the house altogether, go to Page 164.

If you're prefer to go back downstairs and through the doorway, go to Page 233.

To continue down the hall and try the second door on the right, go to Page 304.

To enter the door on the left, go to Page 314.

Four alcoves run along one side of the cathedral, each featuring a set of statues, artwork and, tombs covered by sculpted marble bodies of archbishops and the like. All but one of these are locked behind ornate iron gates, but the last has an open door. The alcoves contain the relics of this church, shards of the cross, bones of saints and apostles, that sort of thing.

There are also thick wooden doors leading to other rooms, presumably church offices and vestries and the living quarters of clergy. When you try one of the doors, you find it locked.

Keep trying doors. Go to Page 327.

Enter the open alcove. Go to Page 336.

The skeleton clearly belonged to a child, and the bones are definitely deformed, misshapen, bulging where they shouldn't be, and even if you're not an expert on anatomy, you're fairly certain there are extra bones where there shouldn't be.

And the bones have been badly scratched.

When you touch one, the bone is Arctic cold, and you can see your next breath.

To leave this small basement, go to Page 213.

To explore the table, go to Page 221.

The whispers aren't a single voice from a single direction. They come from everywhere and anywhere. Some are closer, some further away, some above you, some below, and some inside the middle of your head. They're male and female, old and young, and represent a dozen languages at least. One of the voices belongs to the boy.

One of them is yours.

From the future, or the past, or from some otherwise inaccessible parallel world, you're sending yourself a warning—or something is mimicking you with malevolent intentions. But your own voice doesn't rise above the others, and you cannot discern the words. They're more and more frantic as the source of your own voice falls further away.

"Don't go," you tell yourself, adding your own whisper to the growing cacophony. The other voices grow louder and more persistent. "Shut up," you tell them. For a second, it seems like they listen. All the voices go quiet—but your own voice also dims, so you learn nothing.

The voices rise up again when you move, no matter what direction. After a while, a few steps in any direction is enough to draw the whispers down on you with the full volume of a coliseum. A few more steps, it's like moving through a runway with jets landing and taking off, until another steps causes your ears to bleed, and another causes things inside your head to pulsate and break open.

Eventually, you fall to the floor and listen to the voices—and your own voice saying, "Don't move, not even one step," but it's too late. You've moved. Your ears have dissolved into puddles of blood, and all the blood of your brains spills through them. When you die, you drop the zebra. Eventually, the ghost boy retrieves his toy.

You chose poorly.

The room contains dolls of every type, made of rags and bones and anything else. Some are abstractions, some frighteningly lifelike as though they've trapped someone's soul. They all seem to look at you. You can't tell if they're pleading for release or exceptionally hungry.

They never move when you look at them. But in your peripheral vision, and in the corners of the room you can only hear, there seems to be movement and rustling and tittering.

Some of the dolls are handmade. Others come from every corner of the globe. "You're all very beautiful," you tell the room, perhaps out of a sense of self-preservation, "and I'd love to take you with me, but my car is dead and I'm trying to find my partner."

A low murmur comes in response, unless you only imagine it, unless it's merely the twisted echoes of air moving through vents—are there even vents in a house this old?

At this point, the dolls don't seem to offer any insights, and the room contains nothing else but the spiraling iron staircase and the doorway back to the music room.

To return to the music room, go to Page 160.

To climb the stairs, go to Page 278.

You push at the wall. It feels thin and hollow. You punch it, but one punch is enough to know you'll hurt your fist more than you'll hurt the wall. It may be old, but it's got inertia on its side, and it doesn't seem likely to succumb to mere fists.

You take a trumpet from the wall and swing it like an axe. It howls, the trumpet or the wall, in an inhuman way.

"That," a voice behind you says, "is no way to treat a musical instrument."

When you turn, there's a woman with a flute in her hands. She smiles sadly. She's translucent, though there's little to see but darkness. The candlelight catches inside her rather than reflects off her. She strokes the flute like a cat, but her eyes are on you.

She was young, once, and still shines with youthful radiance, a woman of maybe twenty years, maybe not, but she's out of her time. You can see it clearly in the clothes she wears and her hairstyle and her eyes.

"This was my playroom," she says, using the flute like a baton to take in the entirety of it. "When I was a child, I played in here, and I could make them all sing, every string, every piece of brass, every piece of wood."

She flickers, like the candle, two steps closer in a blink, two more steps, and thrusts the flute upwards through your gut and into your heart. As the pain overtakes you, as you choke on your own blood, as she eases you down toward the floor, you see the woman's father behind her, and her brother, her mother and her sister, all their eyes on you but their expressions revealing different emotions: excitement, sadness, disapproval.

The woman whispers, "They called me a nightingale, sometimes, when I was young, but I suppose I was always young."

Your eyes flutter, your vision fades, and when your sight clears you stare down at your own corpse.

"It's okay," the father says, with all his disapproval. "We'll keep you safe."

John Urbancik

He drags you through the floor to a hole of a basement where he binds your spirit to a brick wall with irons, and despite that you're insubstantial, you're trapped, unable even to rattle the chains.

You chose poorly.

Near the corner of the room, behind an ulna or a radius, you find a small rock you can push. Doing so triggers an internal mechanism. You hear the door sliding, rock against rock, but only when it's too late realize the door has closed behind you, trapping you in a cell less than six feet long. It's just you and a few hundred bones in piles. Try as you might, you cannot trigger the door to open—neither with the same rock or any other. If there's another lever, it's probably on the outside.

Time stretches unknowably. It's impossible to say if you wait for hours or days or years. The bones dance, but that's probably your mind slipping. They play drums on each other, and stage elaborate sword fights, using other bones as props. Eventually, as you waste away, drinking water that reaches you one drop at a time through the stone, rock, and earth, the bones start tapping out their rhythms on your legs and arms and ribs and skull.

Time stretches unknowably until thirst drives you mad and hunger devours you from the inside and consciousness slips mercifully away with your sanity.

You chose poorly.

You retreat to the room with all the statues. The door slams shut of its own accord. Thunder rattles the house. Something skitters in the gloomy shadows. The chandelier fizzles and flickers.

One of the many whispering voices says, "Look out!" One of the statues falls at you.

You manage to get out of the way, but it's close, closer than you would prefer. Some of the voices are laughing. There's no one there to have pushed it, and certainly all of the statues are bottom heavy, their marble plinths a part of the sculptures. It did not fall on its own.

"Watch out!" Another statue tumbles toward you.

"There's no escape!" And another.

It's an effort, to stay out of the way, and you drop the candelabra as you evade the statues. They're coming at you, guiding you in a particular direction, toward an open window you hadn't noticed.

The next falling statue catches your arm, and it's almost enough to knock you to the floor. It's heavy, and it'll probably bruise, and it tears through your clothes and scratches your flesh.

You're at the window now, as far from both doors as you can possibly be, and another statue is slowly tilting in your direction. The voices are now chanting a combination of "Jump!" and "Don't jump!"

Try to get out of the way but stay in the room, go to Page 100.

Try to get out of the way by going out the window, go to Page 290.

You're not really looking for a bathroom, but your lost lover, so instead of following the man's helpful suggestion, you go the other direction. You're tempted to call a name. The hallway is like any other hallway, but it's long, amazingly and impossibly long, and after a while you wonder if you're still in the same place. It stretches forever, though there seems to be an end ahead, a room of some sort. Looking back, you can no longer see the stairs you'd climbed.

Continue forward? Go to Page 263.
Go back? Go to Page 293.

Slowly, careful not to make any sudden move that might be read as hostile, you turn to face the woman who, presumably, has just emerged from the book in your hands. The wax is still under your fingernails.

Very closely, she resembles human. But she's not. Her eyes are too wide apart—and those eyes contain all the green that escaped the book. Her lips are too thin, her cheeks too high, her ears feline. Her hair seems alive, moving and swaying. You say, "Hello."

Slowly, in response, she says the same: "Hell. Low." Then she smiles broadly, revealing just how far from human she is. It's like the smile of a tiger, or a snake, or possibly a demon. She reaches out and touches your cheek gently, like a lover. Her fingers are rough, dry, dusty. She says, in something closer to your language, "You released me."

It's your turn to smile. You're not sure how else to respond.

"You released me," she says again, "and *all* the beasts of the book."

You look down at the book in your hands. Wisps of smoke, tendrils of blue, red, and gold, trail away from it. Behind her, floating in the air, there's a thing like a dragon forming in the shadows, and an eagle with a lion's face, and a man with the head of a jackal, and a bulbous squid with wings, and a wolf with three snarling heads, and a creature that appears to be more teeth than body.

She says, with deliberation, "One. Request."

It's not that she has one, but she's making an offer.

Tell her about your lost lover. Go to Page 110.

Tell her you don't need anything. Go to Page 332.

The harp is heavier than it looks, but with a little muscle, you're able to slide it back into place. The secret panel slides, not quite smoothly, out of the way, revealing another room.

You step into the room, the three candles on your candelabra leading the way. It's about the same size as the music room, but filled with dolls. They sit on the sofas and on the built-in shelves. They stand, where they're able, and they sit clustered together. Their faces are porcelain or cracked leather or stained cloth or sea shell, or faceless dolls made of corn husks blackened by time, and paper-mâché. Paper dolls and bisque dolls and wax dolls sit in elaborate doll houses even though some of the dolls are clearly not of the same scale.

Every single doll face is turned in your direction. All the dolls, dozens or even hundreds of them, stare at you as you enter the room. Behind you, the harp repeats its melody.

An iron spiral staircase ascends from this room. To climb the stairs, go to Page 219.

To stay and explore the doll room, go to Page 269.

John Urbancik

"I can't go away," you tell the boy. "I'm looking for my friend."

The boy pouts. He looks down at his toy animals—a giraffe, an elephant, a tiger—then picks up a zebra and holds it out to you. "I used to have friends," the boy says. "Before the dark nights. Before the whispers."

"Whispers?"

The boy shakes his head. His hand trembles.

Accept the zebra. Go to Page 209.

Continue talking but don't take the zebra. Go to Page 347.

You climb carefully, in case the iron is old and rusted somewhere, but the stairs are solid. The dolls seem sad to see you go. When you look down from halfway up, all their eyes seem to be following your ascent. From the music room, the faint sound of a flute reaches you, as though a breeze gently touches the holes as it passes through the room.

At the top, an iron landing circles the room, which you didn't realize until now is round, with a railing on the outside and a library of books on the inside. Hundreds of books. Thousands. Children's books, mostly, as far as you can tell, illustrated volumes of all the *Wizard of Oz* books, Bibles, ghost stories, fairy tales, devotionals, diaries, natural histories. You can't possibly look at them all, but you glance through them as you circle the room.

There appears to be no doorway.

There must be an exit somewhere, another secret door hidden in the shelves. To look for it, go to Page 216.

To return to the doll room, go to Page 253.

It's a golden chalice, very possibly the Holy Grail itself, or something like it, and maybe it possesses magical attributes. If it can give you insight, maybe you'll be able to find your lover and escape this old spooky house.

The first mouthful tastes like a sweet red wine, but nothing changes. So you drink the rest, all of it, and you wipe the drops that dribbled onto your lips with that back of your hand as you return the chalice to its place.

Nothing seems to happen.

Maybe you should go back to the stairs and rise out of the cellar. Go to Page 90.

Maybe you should look at the book. Go to Page 207.

The crypt is a rectangular room with tombs on the exterior and interior walls. The inside seems to be simpler. Not all of which have names attached. There are those stairs going down on the one side, and on the other, what appears to be a door. It's just stone, and looks no different from any other stone of the cathedral, but it's dug grooves into the floor where it's been swung open over the course of decades or centuries.

It doesn't push open, and there's nothing to grab to pull it open, so there must be some sort of lever. It doesn't take long to find it: there's a lever in the open crypt, but you'll have to crawl all the way in to reach it.

Crawl into the crypt and open that door. Go to Page 355.

Go down those stairs. Go to Page 364.

You don't believe the room has given up all its secrets.

There's a wardrobe, but when you open it, the doors move grudgingly and there's nothing inside but stale air and the odor of moth balls. There's a book on the bed, the cover a faded red with a girl pictured in a circle—Alice, you're sure of it, from *Alice's Adventures in Wonderland*. There's a rag doll on the bed, propped against the pillow, both looking like they've been made of dust and whispers and candlelight.

There's nothing else and no one, so you can look again into the mirror. Go to Page 231.

Or go on to the next room. Go to Page 285.

"No," you say, scrambling away from the dried husk of a man and straight into the next room of the cellar. The demon laughs behind you as you enter a room filled with robed corpses clutching twisted satanic relics, silver crosses as daggers, books bound in human skin and inked with blood, effigies of ancient hellfire godlings. This is the final room of the cellar. There's no place further to go, so you turn to face the demon should it come after you.

For a moment, nothing happens. The demon doesn't pursue you, though you hear him cackling and taunting. "They tried to raise me!" he calls from the other room. "They thought they could control me with salt! *Salt!*"

A line of salt marks the entrance into this room. It's been disturbed, though, probably by you, so there's a break in the barrier. There's also a jar half filled with salt in the hands of one of the former congregants.

Ignore the salt and try to find another way to protect yourself. Go to Page 254.

Restore the line of salt to protect the room. Go to Page 291.

It's a tough climb to the bell tower. The rain-slicked stones threaten to launch you into the night. Unlike the bat, you cannot fly. Finally, you step under the dome of the bell tower and out of the rain. From here, there's only one direction to go: down the dark, narrow stairs.

They wind tightly. The steps are uneven and your shoes are slick, so you hold the stone walls on both sides to prevent an inconvenient slide and tumble.

Down, you descend, dozens of steps then hundreds of steps then thousands. It seems the stairs from the tower never end.

After what feels like forever, finally they end at a thick wood door. You have to put your shoulder to it to force it open.

On the other side, you find yourself in the cloisters, with a garden to one side and the cathedral itself to the other. Beyond the garden is a cemetery, where somebody stands with their back to you.

To go through the garden to the cemetery, go to Page 297.

Or enter the cathedral. Go to Page 342.

The door had closed behind you. It takes effort to push it open, but you leave the sanctuary of the church and return to the storm. It's gotten stronger during the few minutes you were inside. The rain falls redly, the sky above the cathedral is tinted with scarlet, and even the lightning flashes crimson arcs across the sky.

"Leaving so soon?" a voice asks. You don't recognize the voice, but the accent is unexpected, eastern European, perhaps Bulgarian, perhaps Transylvanian.

The man steps out of the darkness like a shadow. He wears a cape. His grin shows his incisors. He says, "I thought perhaps you might join me this night."

Flee. Go to Page 321.

Agree. Go to Page 330.

The next room is another bedroom. Here, there's a girl in the bed. Like the bed, she appears to be made of dust and whispers and candlelight. She looks at you with jaundiced eyes. When you blink, she's not there, the bed is empty, and the thunder from outside seems to be rising in volume.

A window overlooks a cemetery and a church, and you can see a section of the road. There's no indication of life out there. Really, there's no indication of life inside, either.

You step in a puddle of fresh blood on the side of the bed.

Look under the bed. Go to Page 264.

Retreat to the previous bedroom. Go to Page 286.

Run forward, through the next door. Go to Page 292.

You nearly slip in the blood as you make a hasty retreat. It's probably a good thing you moved so quickly. The door to the next room or hall or toilet opens, and you barely catch a glimpse of it as you retreat. Someone screams in agony—someone you never even saw.

But you run straight into a big man with a hammer in one hand, a big man with a hood shrouding his shadowy face, a big man with a free hand that grabs you by the wrist and cracks bone as he lifts you off your feet. You see teeth—they're almost fangs in the dark—and his eyes reflect the candlelight even as the candelabra tumbles to the floor.

He tightens his fist, grinding your bones together, and raises the big hammer. It hardly seems fair, that so large a man would feel any need for so immense a weapon. Briefly, you almost see through him, as though he's not completely there. But the hammer definitely is, as you learn when he brings it down on your head and shatters your skull.

You chose poorly.

You step into the next room, which is darker—there are fewer lights. There are a dozen barrels to both the right and the left, and a tall, gaunt gentleman standing beside one stack of barrels staring back at you. "Who are you?" he asks.

Lie. Go to Page 311.
Tell him the truth. Go to Page 325.

You turn left, primarily because the man below is still watching you and you have to stick to your story. The hall is not as well-lit as the wine cellar, but the woods are rich and luxurious. It's a short hall leading to a door that's slightly ajar. Pushing it open, you hear the shower running, and see steam. You hear what sounds like "La Vie En Rose," and it's utterly beautiful.

If you turn around, go to Page 44

If you enter, go to Page 252.

Outside again, in the storm, you're faced with the same choices you started with.

Walk up to the front door, lift that heavy knocker, and announce yourself. Go to Page 2.

Sneak around the back and climb in through a window. Go to Page 3.

Abandon your partner, friend, and lover, and leave the car and the house. Go to Page 5.

Sit in the front seat of your dead car as the rain pummels its roof. Go to Page 6.

You try to escape the falling statue by climbing out the window. As you get out, something catches you by the neck—a noose which must have been dangling just outside the window and hiding in the dark.

Before you can slip free of the noose, a statue crashes against the wall immediately behind you. You're on a sloped section of the roof, but you're also only a few feet from the edge of it. The dormer offers nothing to grab onto, so you slide forward and over the side. The noose catches you by the neck, cracking it but not immediately killing you. You dangle just out of reach of the roof, so you can't grab it to climb up, and the rope has tightened to suffocate you.

You try to pry it free, but your own weight keeps you trapped. The agony in the bones of your neck prevents you from doing anything heroic. It's only a few minutes before you lose the strength to struggle, and not long after that before you lose consciousness. In the rain, you slip quietly from life.

You chose poorly.

Quickly, you grab the jar of salt. It's a big jar, much bigger than you would use in a kitchen, but the corpse seems unwilling to give it up. The corpse glares at you. The corpse opens its mouth and lets loose a stream of locusts.

They're the largest locusts you've ever heard of, some of them close to three feet in length, with razor edged wings and needles for pincers and antennae.

They swarm you like piranha might swarm a cow trying to crossing their river. It's quick work, actually, so by the time they're gnawing at your bones you no longer feel anything. The demon laughs from the next room until you hear nothing else.

You chose poorly.

You rush out of the bedroom and into the next, a sitting room with a few chairs and an old crib near the window. You nearly slip in the blood, and leave a trail of bloody footprints leading straight to you.

Doors on every room exit this room. All those doors are open, and there's a figure in each. They're all shrouded in darkness, barely reached by the glow of your candelabra. They all turn toward you, though. They all see you clearly. They all carry some sort of weapon—an iron sledgehammer, a slim-bladed dagger, a branding iron.

The door behind you swings shut with a bang. When you reach for the doorknob, you find it's locked itself and refuses to turn.

The man with their weapons advance on you, and there's really no place to run to.

The man with the branding iron asks, "Is it one of ours?"

The man with the sledge says, "It is now."

The man with the dagger reaches you first. You struggle, you drop the candelabra, but he spins you around so he's behind you and pressed tight against you.

"Crush the skull, first," he says to the man with the sledge, "so I can drain the blood."

The hammer is lifted.

The blow is solid and kills you instantly.

You chose poorly.

You turn around and walk, and you walk for a long time, and just as you're beginning to believe you'll walk forever and the hallway will never end, you reach the spiral stairs again. They look slightly different, true, but you can't see exactly how.

You can go on to the promised bathroom. Go to Page 305.

Or go down the stairs again. Go to Page 362.

You get as much of a running start as you can and leap, timing it perfectly to slip between tongues of flame, and land on the other side just through the doorway. For a moment, balance is an issue and you almost fall back, but you right yourself and take a breath and step away from the precipice.

When you look back, the crater rumbles, the ground inside it cracks, and tendrils of flame whip out from underneath. Two of those tendrils wrap around you, burning through the flesh of your legs and chest. The tendrils drag you through the earth into another realm, where demons dance and flames live and spiders are as big as elephants, where the trees have red needle leaves and the grass is slivers of living glass and a giant squid made of fire and smoke and ash has you in its grip. Struggling against it is like trying to resist the sun when it falls on your chest. The thing feeds you into its many-toothed mouth.

You chose poorly.

Down the stairs, the man in the wine cellar waits for you. "Lost again?" he asks.

"It was occupied," you tell him.

"Ah, well, I'm sure there's something we can do. Come this way."

He leads you deeper into the cellar, around the edge of the furthest wine barrels, where there's another door. "It's not as fancy as upstairs," he tells you, ushering you in.

It's a bathroom. It's the idea of a bathroom, at least, with a toilet and a sink and a mirror, but not much more than that. He shuts the door behind you. And he locks it.

If you feel the need to use the facilities, go to Page 317.

Knock on the door and demand release, go to Page 326.

"Your children of the night?" you suggest.

He laughs. "Not mine," he says, "but yes. So tell me, brave soul, what brings you to my door on a night such as this?"

If you feel compelled to make up a story, go to Page 306.

To tell the truth, go to Page 322.

You go through the garden. The rain is relentless, but you're thoroughly soaked already so it makes no difference. Through the garden, its statues and roses, you approach the person at the cemetery.

It's a small plot of land with a few dozen stones, several with cherubs or angels atop them, many with crosses, two or three with statues of saints. When the lightning flashes, you realize the person standing among the stones is actually one of several. They're all looking in your direction, faces pale and teeth sharp.

The children, you realize, of the vampire stranger who left you on the rooftop.

You stop in the clearing between garden and cemetery. The figures are moving—not when you can see them, but between flashes of lightning—changing position, getting closer to you, until the next flash of lightning reveals one right in front of you.

Startled, you jump back into the unmoving chest of another.

With the next flash of lightning, they're on all sides of you, two or three deep now. In the brief darkness between flashes, one bites your throat, another takes your wrist, another goes for the artery in your thigh.

You never have a chance to resist. A dozen vampire children fall on you and drain your blood over the course of three more strikes of lightning, as though that's any way to judge time.

You're not alive for another strike.

You chose poorly.

You fight. You fall into a kind of defensive stance and raise your fists to defend yourself. But she's a vampire, inhumanly strong and unfathomably fast. She drags you to her, drags you the full length of the sacristy until you're under the painting of Jesus. "I like them feisty," she says through bared teeth. Your fists are like bubbles against her. It's like punching raw, dead meat. She buries her teeth in your throat, and touches you in ways you can't comprehend. It's pleasant, this pain, these final breaths, and when it's done she lets you drop to your knees.

"I think I'll keep you a while," she says.

And she does. She keeps you as a slave, as her Renfield, enthralled so that you know what you're doing but can't do anything she doesn't expressly command. She keeps you not just for the night, but for a month, sending you into the woods to gather rats and other vermin, roaches, beetles, spiders, for no reason but her own amusement. She has you consume these things, and she feeds from you whenever she pleases, and you never learn what became of your lover, lost somewhere in this cathedral, imprisoned by the vampire's brother.

For an immortal creature, as she claims to be, she tires of you quickly, and after most of a month, she snaps your neck and disposes of your body.

You chose poorly.

You take off for the front door.

The vampire queen curses under her breath. It's an ancient language, something impossible for your tongue to get around, but you understand it precisely. It stops you. One breath, two, you're not sure what to do next. The shadows are close. The fangs drip. They're in front of you and behind you, above you, at every side. The vampire queen steps closer. "And you told so sad a story," she says, lifting you off your feet.

She drains you at the doors of the church and casts your lifeless body aside for the other, minor vampires to fight over.

You chose poorly.

"I'm looking for someone," you tell him.

He takes a puff on his pipe, sets it on a pipe holder you hadn't noticed earlier, and says, "Tell me everything."

You do. You tell him about the dying car and the rain and your partner disappearing in the darkness. When he asks what you mean by partner, you say lover. He reveals his shock only briefly, then nods and says, "Go on."

"Have you seen anyone?" you ask.

When he approaches you, the pipe and its holder vanish. He looks up and down the length of you, not in any obscene way but with all the awe of a scientist or a child. "I can't say I've seen anyone like you," he says. "I mean, I've seen an ape, and a princess, but you—you've got substance. Depth. Detail." He considers for a moment. "Maybe that one time."

"What one time?" you ask.

He shakes his head. "My mind's getting a bit slippery these days. I'm old, and the opium can be a beast. I've lost entire days, I have. I might have seen someone—someone like you, that is—thirty minutes ago or thirty years ago, I can't be certain."

"Try," you say. "Please."

He nods with determination. "I can do that," he says, but then shakes his head. "This damn headache." He goes to one of the shelves, where a variety of bottles contain pills, powders, and liquids. "Heroin cures everything," he says. "Or is that aspirin?"

A sound catches his attention—a sound you both hear—and you both turn to the doorway where the sound originated. You don't see anything or anyone, but he obviously does. He says, "Anna, what's wrong?" Apparently, she responds. He nods gravely. "Yes, of course. I'll bring the heroin and the laudanum, I'll give you whatever will help best."

You don't see Anna, or anyone else, and looking back to where the man had been standing, you no longer see him or pill bottles, either.

But the door is still there. To go through it, go to Page 234.

To explore the game room more, go to Page 346.

The flames create a wall that prevents any chance of leaping—unless you expect to leap unscathed through unnatural fires—but the crater continues to expand and deepen. You hear the altar in the next room—a solid slab of stone—collapse and slide into the hole, but you never see it.

You cannot see to the bottom anymore.

The crater consumes the bodies of the congregants. They tumble in and disappear as you edge back into the last, most distant corner.

No rescue is coming. There's no other exit. When the ground beneath you crumbles, you tumble into the hole. You try not to fall, but the ground inside the crater is like sand. There's nothing to grab hold of. The flames dance around you as you plummet through a void, through a fiery obscurity. The fall never ends. The fires dance around you and prick randomly at your skin.

Somewhere, the demon cackles, and you know you've lost.

The cackling follows you through eternity.

You chose poorly.

The wine cellar is actually a maze of wine bottles and columns and drinking stations with marble tabletops and ornate wine openers. Every column has a face carved into the top of it, a face like a grotesque, variations of what might have once been human or fairy or demonic.

After a while, you realize you've gotten thoroughly lost, wandering halls full of wine without end. When you finally find a staircase and climb it, you emerge in a restaurant in another country, before opening, as chefs and servers are preparing for the day's service.

They're confused to find you there. You don't speak their language, and they don't speak yours. There's no way back to the old spooky house, and your lover is possibly lost forever.

You chose poorly.

The last door on the right opens onto a small bedroom. There's a bed meant for a child, and a small desk under the window. The bookshelf holds a selection of children's books from decades past. Some of them look familiar, but they're covered with a thick coating of dust and a spider's web occupied by something the size of a tarantula. It stares at you and challenges you to take one of its books. It's got a hundred little eyes and coarse black hair and fangs dripping with venom.

You step away from the bookshelf.

There's a chair next to the bed, as though someone had sat there so regularly, and this was its normal spot.

There was a mirror in this room, on the back of a bureau, but it was shattered long ago, and the shards have been cleaned up. All that remains is the black wood backing and the hole made by someone's fist. It had been cleaned up, but never repaired.

Briefly, you see a reflection anyhow, as though the frame of the mirror is occupied by the ghost of itself. The image shows a woman seated beside a child. She holds the child's hand. A man behind her puts his hand on her shoulder. Everyone wears black suits, dresses, and veils, and the room is crowded with mourners.

The room is, of course, empty. There's no mirror, and there's no reflection.

There's nothing else in this room, and certainly no sign of your missing partner. You hurry out. To go downstairs and into the office, go to Page 142.

If you'd rather go downstairs and leave the house altogether, go to Page 164.

If you'd prefer to go back downstairs and through the doorway, go to Page 233.

To go back down the hall and try the first door on the right, go to Page 265.

To enter the door on the left, go to Page 314.

You continue forward. The hall is not as well-lit as in the other direction, but the woods are just as rich and luxurious, and this time it's a short hall leading to a door that's slightly ajar. Pushing it open, you hear the shower running, and see steam. You hear what sounds like "La Vie En Rose," and it's utterly beautiful.

You can enter. Go to Page 252.

Or turn around and return to the cellar. Go to Page 362.

"I'm fascinated by cathedrals," you tell him. He's still holding you in place, which is probably good—the slope is steep, and the way down is long and ends abruptly. "I didn't know this one was...occupied."

He laughs. It's a wicked laugh, even more so with the thunder punctuating it. "There are always ghosts," the stranger says. Then he adds, "Or beasts of some sort. I'm probably a little bit of both."

"I can just be on my way," you say. "I didn't mean to disturb you."

"Don't you at least want a photograph?" the stranger asks. "You've come so far."

"It's a terrible night for photography," you tell him.

"All nights are terrible," he tells you. Then he shakes his head. "Would you consider yourself my guest?"

Do not presume. Go to Page 323.

Accept. Go to Page 360.

The dining table could easily sit twenty. There are, in fact, only five there now, sitting around what appears to be a grand display of meat. It's not cooked meat, the odor is rather foul, and you're not sure you want to know where it came from or what it was when it was alive.

You realize the smell isn't only coming from the meat on the table. The diners themselves are in various stages of rot, with wounds under their clothes that you didn't immediately notice, wounds still bloody or festering.

One looks up at you and says, quite distinctly, "Brains."

They all look at you. They look hungry, even as they eat. But they are eating, and they're not making any move to involve you in any way.

The zombie from the freezer blocks your exit. The only other possibility is to go forward, but the new arrival has attracted the attention of the diners. And they've all focused their teeth on you.

You try to fight, but your punches are ineffective. Even Rocky could never defeat chunks of raw meat. You try to run, but there's no way to get past them all, and their grips are vices you can't escape.

Their teeth are dull but persistent, and they're not adverse to tearing their meat right off the bones—even when you're still alive.

You don't remain alive for long.

You chose poorly.

She walks you out into the cathedral. The eyes of paintings shift to watch the two of you. Shadows move to get a better view. Statues turn their heads. The man praying in the pews watches, as well, out of the corner of his eyes.

When she walks, her heels make a thunderous staccato on the marble floor. The outside thunder seems to have quieted in deference to the woman escorting you through the cathedral. Things crawl in the dark, things skitter and scamper, either to make a path or to more clearly see.

She holds herself regally, yes, but perhaps it's more than that. She pauses briefly to smile at you. With her eyes, she tells you to look to the altar. And there, in a place where you thought there had been a statue of Jesus, it's actually her. This isn't a Christian cathedral at all, but one devoted to the woman walking with you now. The statue wears a crown of thorns, but the face, you now see, is clearly female, and clearly hers.

You open your mouth and take a breath to ask a question, but let it die on your lips. Perhaps it's best not to know too many answers.

As you walk, the cathedral seems smaller, as though the walls themselves, and the vaulted ceilings, are leaning close to see what will happen.

She leads you to a stone door, then stands aside to allow you to enter. "That way," she says, "and good luck." Then she winks and says, "I believe in you. *I believe in love.*"

Go through the door. Go to Page 328.
Don't. Go to Page 357.

It's a long walk away from the alcove. You don't feel comfortable with your back to it. There are eyes in the shadows. You reach the doors you entered through without incident. A quick glance reveals the man still kneeling there near the front row of pews.

Go to Page 284.

"I was looking for a book," you tell her, glancing quickly at the stack of them at her side.

She rises far more agilely than her ancient, dusty bones suggest is possible. "This is not a library," she says, coming closer, "and you should not lie in the presence of greater powers."

She compels you to retreat, into the passage, but you quickly realize the marble door had closed without a sound behind you. There's barely room to turn around. The old woman at the other edge of the passage prevents you from moving forward. She's shaking her head. "I can tell you much about the *Books of Blood*," she tells you. "Or perhaps *The Book of Lost Fates*. There was an entry about you. I read it just today. *Blood shall be a Feast*, or so it was written."

She seems too big to get through the passage, but she enters. Her teeth are too big for her mouth. There's no further retreat, and no room to fight, but you do the best you can as she grabs at you with clawed fingers and, unaffected by your feeble attempts to defend yourself, ravages your body, shredding skin and gulping blood, sighing and moaning as she does so, practically hyperventilating, as though she doesn't often get a chance to feed like this.

You chose poorly.

"I'm just looking for the bathroom and made a wrong turn," you tell him.

"Of course you have." He doesn't believe it. He's staring down at you along a long, crooked nose. His eyes twitch. "Well, then, if you would follow me." He leads you around the edge of the cellar room to a spiral stairway. "This leads straight up to the main hall. You'll find facilities to the left."

He gestures for you to climb the stairs, merely watches you climb. At the top, a door leads to a hall, and you can go either to the left or right.

To go right, go to Page 274.

To go left, go to Page 288.

You tell her quickly about your car, dead on the side of the road, and the storm and the house, and your partner, missing in the dark. When you're done, she says, "I must remain here, with my books, but I wish you luck." She smiles. It's sincere. But there are too many teeth for her mouth. She indicates the passage you took to arrive, and with some trepidation, you exit.

The door closes behind you when you've returned to the crypt.

Or you can go up the way you came and maybe check out the alcoves. Go to Page 335.

You can go down the stairs, deeper beneath the crypt. Go to Page 364.

"Thank you," you say, "but I ought to find my lover myself, don't you think?"

She smiles. It's a pretense. It's temporary, and already faltering. "I believe in love," she says. "I believed it in so thoroughly, look what's become of me now." She spreads her arms in a sudden movement, raising them on either side, bringing the dress to life as though it's the wings of a bat, revealing her sharp teeth and blood red lips and eyes that glow crimson.

"You," she says, moving forward, "are not worthy of love."

Fight. Go to Page 298.
Flee. Go to Page 339.

The left door opens onto what appears to be the master bedroom. An enormous bed sits centered against the far wall, but it doesn't dwarf the room. There are two desks near the two windows, each closed and shuttered against the storm. On one of the desks, a candle burns, and a half written letter lays open beneath an old fountain pen.

The pen has dried out.

The letter says: *I fear the worst. It's my mind, not my children. It's all in my head. No one is ill but me, and I cannot escape it. Oh, sister, I wish you could spare the time to visit, but with your husband's suicide—I know that's what they say—I fear you'll never*

It ends midsentence. There's a fat drop of ink after that, directly under the nib of the pen. It's dry, dry and fading, flaking away like memories lost to the wind.

A large dresser dominates one wall. There's a brush with long strands of blonde hair stuck between the bristles and an ivory handled mirror.

The ceiling is arched, rising well over the room. The architectural elements are complex, dividing the ceiling into a number of panels, each of which has been painted with separate scenes. A dancing bear. A storm cloud that mirrors the clouds presently crowding the sky outside. Aphrodite rising from a shell on the shore. A giant squid capsizing a large sailing vessel. A king in yellow on his throne. In some panels, the colors are vibrant. It's obvious different artists worked on different images.

"Have you seen the color of the moon?" she asks.

She's not there, so her whispered question wasn't real, just a figment of your imagination, an echo of a question asked of someone else from distant decades.

But she asks again. "Is it the color of madness?"

There's nothing else in this room, and certainly no sign of your missing partner. You hurry out. To go downstairs and into the office, go to Page 142.

If you'd rather go downstairs and leave the house altogether, go to Page 164.

If you'd prefer to go back downstairs and through the doorway, go to Page 233.

To try the first door on the right, go to Page 265.

To go down the hall and try the last door on the right, go to Page 304.

You make a run for it.

You won't get far, not in those handcuffs, but you at least make it out of the courtroom and out of the courthouse and onto the street of the small town. The roads are dusty, even with puddles, and the sun is bright.

You run one way or another, but the police are already giving chase. It doesn't take long to reach the edge of town, but you'd run much quicker without those handcuffs.

If you have Harry Houdini level lock picking and escape artist skills, go to Page 37.

If you do not, go to Page 45.

Ah, now don't you feel better?

The light, a single naked bulb, already dim, flickers. In the flickering, you see a figure in the mirror behind you.

When you turn, the light goes out entirely. Whoever—or whatever—is in the cellar bathroom with you shoves your head back against the mirror. The light flickers on again, and you see the smile—only the smile, an inhuman crack on a porcelain white face that's nearly perfectly round. There's a splash of blood—fresh blood, your blood—on that face.

You try to fight, but it smashes your head back a second time with inhuman strength. When its mouth opens, when that smile cracks the porcelain and tips the back of it open, its laughter is the sound of a million souls writhing in agony.

The light goes out one last time. Your own lights follow.

You chose poorly.

It's a long walk down the full length of the cathedral. The shadows follow you. The statuary—and there's plenty of it, saints and martyrs and angels—seems to follow your progress. Every step echoes. The high, vaulted ceilings amplify your footsteps so they're almost as robust as the thunder outside.

The person sitting there must hear you, but gives no indication that they do. By the time you reach the row of pews, you know that man is not your partner. The tricky shadows give him similar dimensions, perhaps, at least from a distance, but now that you're closer you feel foolish for ever having considered it.

He looks to you, then with a nod suggests you should join him.

You approach, and when you're close enough to speak, he indicates you should kneel beside him. When the two of you are kneeling, and both facing the altar, he says in a whisper, "You shouldn't be here."

"Why not?"

"This is no holy place," the man says. "It never was. *They* built it."

"*They?*"

"The vampires."

He lets the word hang there. He remains still, doesn't even look at you, and finally adds "My family—they've taken all of them." A tear runs lonely down his cheek. You're surprised you can see it in these shadows. "They won't let me leave. They won't let *you* leave, now, either."

"What do you suggest?" you ask. You're here for a reason, of course, but you don't tell him. You don't ask what reason he had, if any. You don't even know if you should believe him.

"If I rise," he says, "if I try to get to the door, they'll pounce on me. They'll shatter another of my toes or ribs or fingers." You glance at his hands, folded before him as though in prayer. The fingers are entirely misshapen and swollen and stained with what might be old, unwashed blood. "I am to remain in prayer until they're ready for me, that's what they told me. I'm ready now, I think. I'm ready, I don't want to be here anymore, but they only reward me with *pain*."

You don't say anything. What can you say? Can you offer solace, or promise salvation?

"If you can leave," he says, "you *must*."

"Not without my partner," you say. It's barely a whisper. You didn't mean to say it aloud.

He squeezes his eyes closed. "I understand. I do." He shakes his head once. "This isn't the place. But—there's a crypt, sometimes they keep their prey there." Quickly, his eyes indicate a door in the column in the middle of the center aisle. "And a sacristy." He swallows and lowers his head. There's another tear. "I'd pray for you, but I'm not sure it's appropriate, not here."

That's the point when you realize the statue of Jesus at the alter does not, in fact, resemble any version of Jesus you've seen before.

Go to the crypts. Go to Page 206.

Go to the alcoves and doors that may lead to the sacristy. Go to Page 266.

Or leave the cathedral. Go to Page 343.

Among the corpses, you find nothing else. The stink of them begins to permeate your lungs and skin and soul. It's a terrible thing. You realize the black robes are actually not black at all, but covered with a black mold that's now spread onto your own clothes and the skin of your hands where you held the dagger.

The weapon itself is ornate, a series of arabesques dancing around each other, the arms of someone being crucified twisted around the cross. It is not, however, a Christian figure but something else.

You search, hoping perhaps for a lever to open a secret door that would reveal some sort of treasure or, even better, your lost partner and lover. As you explore, discovering nothing useful, the crater formed by the collapse of the demon expands.

When you finally notice it, the crater has stretched to block the entrance, and is several feet deep and wide. You might be able to jump it, but as you watch a crack forms in the bottom and tongues of flame reach out, licking the cellar ceiling and shattering the lightbulb.

The lights in the adjacent rooms and hall also pop, one after the other. You hear them all dying even as the crater expands and deepens. The flames dance through the hole.

If you think you can make the leap, go to Page 294.

If you don't think so, you can wait and see what happens. Go to Page 302.

You don't get a single step before the stranger enfolds you in his cape, in his arms, in his grip. He drags you up, straight up the side of the cathedral, to the steep roof of one of the bell towers. He holds you in place, looking down at a ground you barely see through the murk. The rain pummels you.

He pauses as a wolf howls in the distance. He points beyond the house, toward a town not too far away. "Ah," he says. "What music."

Converse. Go to Page 296.
Resist. Go to Page 367.

You tell him. You admit you're not brave, but you're without choice. Your partner, your lover, has gone missing after your car died and your phone refused to work, so what choice did you have?

The stranger nods. "Admirable," he says in his thick accent. "My children run rampant throughout this cathedral. They are like ticks, I tell you. I shan't assist you, but also I shan't get in your way." He gestures toward one of the bell towers. "Stairs there will bring you down from the roof. If your lover is in this building, you should begin by getting inside."

Then the stranger, the vampire, transforms before your eyes into the shape of a bat. He takes off into the rain, into the storm and away from the cathedral—away, too, from the old house.

Climb to the bell tower he suggested and descend. Go to Page 283.

Or, assuming he's lying, go instead to the other bell tower. Go to Page 348.

"I wouldn't presume such a thing," you tell the stranger. "I know I'm an unwanted intruder on a stormy evening."

"It's merely a storm," the stranger says. "A bit of lightning. A bit of thunder. Well, if you shan't be my guest, then I have no duty to protect you."

"Protect me?"

He lets go of you.

You maintain your balance for a moment on the steep rooftop, but it's precarious, and the wind whips around you and threatens to throw you over the edge.

Thunder booms, the rain goes cold, and the stranger—the vampire—is gone, leaving you alone on the rooftop.

Maybe he'll return. If you want to wait, go to Page 331.

If you want to try to climb to the nearest bell tower, where there may be stairs, go to Page 354.

"Sure," you say, bending slightly to get closer to their level. "What game have you got in mind?"

The children look at each other again, then turn to you. "A good one, of course," the boy says.

"A game of blood," the girl says.

They leap at you simultaneously. They're small, but fast, and impossibly strong. Their nails are like razors. They slash at you, cutting deeply, burying their teeth in your legs and back. You drop backwards, trying to reach a weapon of some sort — one of those chisels, perhaps — but they drag you to the marble floor. Once they've got you down, there's no getting up again — until someone else steps into the room and says, "Children."

They leap immediately off you, holding their hands behind their backs in some gesture of innocence, though the girl takes a moment to wipe your blood from her mouth. They look at the newcomer, a man who might be their father, whose eyes are so blue they glow.

Find a weapon. Go to Page 259.

Wait and see what happens. Go to Page 359.

You tell the man your name and your story, about the dead car on the side of the road, the dead mobile phone, the old spooky house—you're in the basement of that house now—and your partner, your lover, inexplicably missing.

"There's no one in the house," the man tells you. "There hasn't been in over thirteen years. If there were, I'd hear every footstep echoing through the floorboards. Trust me on this."

You might, you might not. He adds, "You should try the church."

He leads you through the wine cellar to a spiral staircase, down a hall, and finally out onto the porch. There, in the same direction as your car, is a church, visible only from the other direction so you never saw it as you approached the house. Lightning dances around its spires.

It's of the same kind of structure and material as the house, and looks no less promising. But it seems a more likely destination for your partner than a dark house in the middle of nowhere—admittedly, the church is also dark and in the middle of nowhere, but that's semantics.

You can sneak around the back, climb in through a window, perhaps conduct a search without alerting the house's residents to your presence. If so, go to Page 3.

You can abandon your partner, friend, and lover, and leave the car and the house. If so, go to Page 5.

You can explore the church. If so, go to Page 9.

You pound on the bathroom door. "Let me out!" you call.

But there's no answer, not even the echo of an answer, no hint of any sound coming from the other side of the door.

Eventually, the single naked bulb goes out.

No matter how much you try, you cannot unlock the door, or wiggle it open, or move it at all. After a time, you try to break the door down, but it's stronger than your shoulder and stronger than your leg. You only hurt yourself.

You sit alone in the dark bathroom, the only sound an occasional drip of water or rattling in the pipes. You try knocking and pounding on the walls and ceiling, you try running the sink—no water comes out—you scream until you're hoarse, but no one and nothing responds.

In time, you weaken.

In time, you're allowed to sit with your thoughts, and they slip into the surreal as you suffer hunger and dehydration. In the darkness, you see the shapes of whispers, and hear the shadows like owls flying close, and maybe one time, maybe twice, you manage to catch a spider in the corners, but the spiders provide little by way of nutritional value.

Time kills you slowly, but it kills you nonetheless.

You chose poorly.

You open the left door. For a moment, the knob resists, but then it turns and the door swings open to reveal a game room. There's stacks of old board games—very old board games, like Draughts, Cribbage, the World's Fair Game and Voice of the Mummy, Go, and the Game of the British Empire. There are decks of cards—regular playing cards, tarot cards, other cards more bizarre—and dice made of metal, wood, and possibly bone.

The room is dominated by a billiards table. Three balls remain on the table, as well as two cues, and a fair amount of dust. Its red felt looks matted and lifeless. Around it, there are several tables to play the games, and a variety of notepads—presumably for keeping score but now bordering on disintegration—and pencils.

There's a Ballyhoo—some kind of pinball table without flippers but numerous pegs inside for bouncing the metal balls—on one of the tables.

Also, there's the distinctly sweet smell of pipe smoke.

A man sits at one of the tables staring at you. He uses a match to re-light his pipe, takes a deep breath of the smoke, and says, "Looks like you've seen a ghost."

If you want to give him a smartass answer, go to Page 260.

If you'd rather tell him the truth, go to Page 300.

You grasp the knob, turn it, open the door, and walk through.

For a moment, you're not sure where you are. You're outside the cathedral. You're in the rain again, under the violent storm. The lightning dances around you. She closes the door behind you. In front of you, the old spooky house sits on the hill, and the cemetery waits off to the side.

Walk up to the front door, lift that heavy knocker, and announce yourself. Go to Page 2.

Sneak around the back and climb in through a window. Go to Page 3.

You can enter through the cellar doors in the back. There's a lock in place, but it's open so you don't have to break in. If so, go to Page 4.

Go to the cemetery. Go to Page 365.

You enter the cemetery.

Briefly, the storm shudders. Thunder explodes more violently than you've heard it, and the display of lightning brightens the sky like a nuclear blast. After that, the rain ends abruptly. The wind dies down. Two steps, three steps into the cemetery, you see a shadow laying on the grass in front of one of the stones, between the massive granite headstone and a smaller footstone.

The headstone has a name etched onto it. Yours.

Best to ignore it.

The shadow wakes, stretching arms and rising to a sitting position, and quickly sees you standing there. Your partner. Your lover. Lost in the storm and soaking wet.

"What did I miss?"

You run to your partner, embrace, kiss, spend far more time than is advisable in this particular graveyard, then walk through the remnants of the storm to your car. When you turn the key, the engine starts right up as if nothing was ever wrong with it. You and your lover drive away from the spooky old house on the hill, the cathedral, and the cemetery as the first red line of dawn touches the eastern horizon.

Congratulations. You chose well.

"Of course I might," you tell the stranger. "That was always my intention."

"Was it, now?" He steps closer. "It's a terrible night to be out in the rain. Perhaps you would like to—come inside?" He pushes open the door, pushes it easily, as though there's no weight, and gestures you inside.

If you want to enter the cathedral again, go to Page 256.

Or you can run. Go to Page 367.

You wait.

The storm doubles down. The wind grows stronger, the rain sharper, the lightning more frenetic, and everything's red.

You wait, but you don't wait long.

A voice says, "I can see you."

Her voice comes from below. You peer over the edge of the cathedral rooftop and see a woman in a long red dress hanging, upside down so most of the dress flows beneath her head and, though it reveals the shape of her, still manages to cover her completely.

She smiles.

You lose your balance.

She catches you. Her grip is tight, and maybe she breaks a few ribs, and then she's breaking the skin of your throat as she bites.

It's strangely erotic, and breathtaking, and terrifying all at the same time. She doesn't drink every drop of blood, but when she licks her lips and smiles wetly in your face again, you're light-headed and having difficulty focusing.

She says, "Oops." Then she lets you go.

You fall, headfirst, and don't survive the landing.

You chose poorly.

Looking around at the expanding menagerie, you say, not loudly, "I don't need anything."

"Then we are freed," the woman says. She steps forward and wraps an arm around you to pull you close. For a moment, you think she's going to kiss you—you're not quite sure how that would work—but that's not it at all. She lifts you off the grated iron walkway around the library and floats into the air above the room of dolls.

Then the other creatures, two dozen of them or more, attack the house in every direction. They tear into the walls and rip through the ceiling. You hear glass shattering, now that the thunder has paused, and you hear things crashing through floors. Something splashes, and apparently a fight of some sort ensues on the shore of a lake hidden within the house—it makes no sense to you, all the noises, the screams of ghosts being torn asunder, ghouls shrieking in terror, church bells going mad. Right down the middle, the house cracks. The crack expands and widens and shatters everything in its path.

The creatures ravage the house. Windows shatter. Rooms collapse. Fires erupt. The night sky breaks open like a spider's web. The house comes tumbling down, with the woods around it, a church, a town. Even your car breaks apart.

The woman gently lands you in a clear spot at the center of this unnatural storm. In the end, not a single wall of the house remains standing. There are bodies, too many bodies to count, some of them grotesque things you've never imagined. The creatures of the *Bestiarum Vocabulum* scatter into the night, leaving you alone amid the ruins.

Through the ruins, you search for any sign of your partner and lover, your companion this night, swallowed first by the storm or the house, now ripped apart by the creatures you'd unleashed, as dead as dead can be, not a drop of blood un-spilt.

You're not dead. Maybe that's a good thing. You hear the sounds of destruction spreading in every direction. You still hold the wax-sealed book. Its creatures still emerge, turning the pages on their own, crawling out of the book, slithering into the darkness and burrowing into the earth.

The wax burns under your fingernails.

You chose poorly.

You go forward, trying to give the dead diners plenty of room to go about their business. It crosses your mind that they might be consuming your partner and lover, but they seem to have made some progress on the—you insist on calling it *meat*—too much so for the short amount of time you've been separated.

They chew loudly. Smack their lips. Tear at the flesh. Crack bones between their teeth. And just as you're slipping past, right up against the wall as far from them as you can get, one spins around and goes in for a hug.

It's a bear hug.

It's a crushing bear hug, and one of the others comes in, as well, as the first buries its teeth in your flesh.

The one who had spoken before, who had so eloquently said, "Brains," says it again, perhaps because it's the only word it knows.

They drag you onto the table, and the five of them abandon their current course for the fresh meat.

You chose poorly.

Emerging from the crypts, you see the man still kneeling in prayer before the altar, but you go the other direction, toward the alcoves running along one side of the church.

Go to Page 266.

The alcove contains one marble tomb, the name of its resident etched into a golden plaque. A dozen narrow carvings represent various figures important to the church in general and to this cathedral in particular, though upon closer examination it appears none of these are the saints and cardinals you might have expected. Instead, they're beasts, subtle variations of humanity, with elongated teeth, lupine or vulpine, eyes too big or too wide or carved with almond-shaped irises like cats or snakes.

The dominant painting in this alcove appears normal, until you realize it features a trickle of blood at the corner of the mouth. The eyes are the same red.

This isn't, you realize, a Christian cathedral.

To leave the cathedral, go to Page 309.

To return to the main part of the cathedral and approach the person praying at the front, go to Page 318.

To explore the doors and maybe find one that's open, go to Page 327.

The next room contains more cabinets and drawers, more paintings, more sculptures grouped haphazardly throughout the room. It's a workshop of some sort, with tools like chisels and paintbrushes and buckets of mortar.

Two children sit at a table. They're so still, you at first think they are statues. They watch you, only their eyes moving, even as you approach them.

They're dressed in their Sunday best, the boy in a tiny suit, the girl in a fluffy dress. You say, "Hello."

They look at each other, smile, then transfer that smile to you. There are too many teeth, all jagged and sharp and bloody.

"We just want to play," the girl says.

"Won't you play with us?" the boy asks.

If you want to play, go to Page 324.

If you don't, go to Page 351.

You tell her about your partner, your lover, missing since your car died alongside the spooky old house on the hill and this impossible cathedral hidden behind the trees. You admit your mobile phone refuses to work and you don't really know where you are. She listens attentively and does not interrupt. When you finish, she says, "That sounds truly dreadful, it does. I lost my love once, long ago, in a cathedral not unlike this." Then she smiles, and she touches your hand, a consoling gesture, though you never realized she was that close to you. "I believe I can help."

She tells you about another visitor, recently arrived, within the past hour or less, whom her brother has led to a particular chapel within the cathedral. "I can bring you there," she says. "Reunite you."

Accept her offer. Go to Page 308.
Refuse. Go to Page 313.

You run. You run the full length of the sacristy and almost reach the door before she's directly ahead of you, arriving so fast you can hardly comprehend it. You run straight into her and bounce back. You land on your butt.

"You're a fool," she says, baring her teeth again and hissing before falling on you and tearing your throat open.

She feeds on your blood for longer than you remain alive.

You chose poorly.

"I'll worship you until dusk falls upon humanity," you say, though you're not quite sure where the words come from. They spill from your mouth of their own accord. "Until the sun expands to swallow the earth, I will worship you, and I will guide your followers like a shepherd until their feet are bloody and their throats parched by the desert, and I will give unto you all of their flesh and all of their blood until the end of time itself."

Her smile grows, but her eyes look behind you. "Such sweet words," she says. "Brother, did you fashion those words?"

A man behind you admits, "I did."

She shakes her head. "Pity." She snaps your neck so quickly, it hardly even hurts. She says something then to her brother, something you cannot properly hear or comprehend, something about another visitor in the cathedral, but by the time your body drops to the floor you're already dead.

You chose poorly.

You hesitate, and don't let the author approach. You ask, "How do I know it will end happily ever after?"

"Happily ever after," the author tells you, "is a lie. There's always a sequel."

You know the story in the book is the story of this old spooky house—specifically, the story of the old spooky house as it is this very moment. "Will I find my partner?"

The author shakes his head. "I'm sorry, your partner is lost to you forever. At least in this life. Now move aside, I have a story to finish."

You refuse to accept such an ending. You say, "No." You do not move aside.

"Fine," the author says. Then he stabs you with the sharp edge of the pen. It's swift, as though he's spent the past twenty years practicing this very specific move. The nib breaks through the skin of your throat precisely, and a second time, so that he cuts open arteries and windpipe.

"It might have been nicer," the author tells you, holding and guiding you as you drop to the ground, "but your story was already at an end."

As you bleed out and suffocate, the author calmly walks to the book, removes and replaces the nib on his fountain pen, and writes the final three words of your story.

You chose poorly.

You enter the cathedral from the other side, so that the alcoves and doors are on either side of you, a wall straight ahead, the sanctuary and altar to your left, and a single person kneeling in the front pew.

Explore the doors and alcoves. Go to Page 266.

Or approach that person, who may or may not be your partner. Go to Page 318.

It's a long walk away from the altar. You don't feel comfortable, with your back to the front of the building. It feels like there are eyes in the shadows, and the man's words echo inside your head. Finally, you reach the doors you entered through, without incident. You glance quickly toward the man still kneeling near the front row of pews.

Go to Page 284.

As you explore, you find exactly what you expect in the cabinets. None of the paintings seem to reveal hidden doorways. There are no additional openings under the big table, at least not any you can find. Two tall, narrow windows flank the painting of Jesus. There's a lot of ironwork there, and the panes are brilliantly colored but the images abstract. They don't allow you to see anything outside except the flickering lightning.

On the wall above the door you came through, there's another painting, a scene of the last supper, very dark and brooding. You don't recognize the artist or the particular image, but you recognize the scene.

"Beautiful, isn't it?" a woman asks.

She steps out of the shadows. The room is awash with shadows, but you'd moved through several. If you had seen her, you'd thought she was a statue. Even now, looking directly at her, you could be convinced she's not real. The darkness desaturates all color, so she might be a slab of marble. Even her dress, thin and wispy and light, seems perfectly still though the slightest breeze should make it dance. It only moved when she did. Her accent is European, perhaps French, perhaps Spanish. "Is there something I can help you with?"

Tell her the truth. Go to Page 338.

Lie to her. Go to Page 352.

You go for the door. But it's too late. The vampire queen has given you your chance, and you ignored it. She holds the door now and says, simply, "No." With one hand, she keeps it shut, and before you can do anything else, a swarm of vampires descend from the darkness. There are more than you can count, more maybe than should be able to live in a small town, an endless sea of vampiric faces rushing in to take a quick taste of your blood.

One drops after another, from your throat and shoulder and chest and back and legs and arms and wrists and mouth. The vampires ravage you, one tiny bite at a time, one drop of blood at a time, until there's nothing left inside you.

At that point, the vampire queen holds you up by your throat. She says, "Stay with me a little longer, won't you?" You haven't got the strength to respond. You're not even sure why you aren't dead yet. These are the last vestiges of consciousness.

She rips open her own wrist and feeds you.

The blood is hot and salty and sweet. The first drop invigorates you. You find yourself greedily slurping down more, as much as you can get. Your body sheds its humanity, with no small amount of agony, as you transform into something else, something subservient to the vampire queen.

When your eyes open next, you're a vampire.

What happens next is a story for another time.

You chose wrongly.

On one of the shelves, you find an old Ouija board, a rectangle of wood with the alphabet in two rows, a row of numerals, *Yes* next to a circle and *No* next to a star and moon on the top corners, stars in the bottom corners, *Good Bye* along the bottom. At the top, it says Trademarked and Registered. There's no planchette. No fancy illustrations. The wood looks well used and rough, as likely to give splinters as speak with spirits.

There's an iron delivery truck about six inches long, hints of the original reds still visible and not a spot of rust, and a set of wooden dominoes in a small wood box.

On one of the tables, you find a ring, possibly an engagement ring, very small, a silver band with a tiny diamond—it might be a real diamond—in a swirl of arabesques.

Take the ring. Go to Page 229.

Leave the ring and go through the door to the next rom. Go to Page 234.

You don't take the offered zebra. "Thanks, but I better not," you tell the boy. "What's your name?"

But the boy isn't there anymore. Neither are the other toys, just the painted zebra that clatters on the floor. Instead of the boy, you hear the whispers. They're distant, at first, and impossible to understand, but they're persistent and getting louder. Not just louder, but insistent, and angry, and cacophonous.

The whispers strike you from the inside, tearing at your ears and at your brains. Behind it all, you hear the boy crying, and maybe it's the boy screaming, too, you can't be sure. The noise is terrible and internal. Your ears bleed. You drop the candelabra, losing most of your light—there's still the staccato of lightning. The voices belong to no one anywhere but inside your head. They pound at the insides of your skulls and behind your eyes. They tear at your tongue. They rip their way through brain matter and tissue and muscle and blood.

As the voices scramble your insides, you fall over, bleeding from the ears and eyes, and the last thing you see is the boy. After setting your candelabra right, he picks up the fallen zebra, and he looks at you with the saddest eyes until the whispers drown out your ability to draw breath.

You chose poorly.

It's a tough climb to the bell tower. The rain-slicked stones threaten to launch you into the night. Unlike the bat, you cannot fly. Finally, you step under the dome of the bell tower and out of the rain. From here, there's only one direction to go: down the dark, narrow stairs.

They wind tightly. The steps are uneven and your shoes are slick, so you hold the stone walls on both sides to prevent an inconvenient slide and tumble.

Down, you descend, dozens of steps then hundreds of steps then thousands. It seems the stairs from the tower never end.

After what feels like forever, finally they end at a thick wood door. You have to put your shoulder to it to force it open.

On the other side, you discover a crypt.

Fires in sconces light the crypt, which contains the final remains of a dozen or more priests, bishops, and saints. Several blocks of marble have names engraved on them, but many are empty and one is open.

The open tomb is empty.

The ceiling is high here, but not as high as inside the cathedral. The lights are dim and the shadows thick, and someone — or something — breathes in the darkness.

It's your partner.

You run to embrace. Too late, you see your lover's incisors have changed, sharpened and lengthened, and they're buried in your neck before you can react.

Your partner drags you in. You — you try to resist, but you're not that strong, and you've already lost blood. Your lover shoves you bodily into the crypt and closes it, locking you in eternal darkness.

Within the marble crypt, you're unable to see, you hear nothing — not even the scratching of others imprisoned alive within these walls. Your lover returns intermittently to feed on you, keeping you weak, until eventually you're not strong enough to even acknowledge your lover's arrival. Eventually, even those visits stop, and your mind wanders through surreal landscapes in an attempt to make sense of impossible mysteries before death finally welcomes you.

You chose poorly.

You run.

It seems the only sane thing to do.

You run past the old man and into the chapel. You don't get far. The diners in their fancy dress are faster than you, and the chef himself lifts you off your feet. "Excellent," he says again, carrying you—no matter how you flail or struggle or try to fight—through the dining room and into a makeshift kitchen. He wraps you with ropes and gags you and marinates you with something that might be blood.

After ten minutes of prep, he puts you on a platter and brings you out to the dining room, where thirteen sacrilegious diners wait. He sets you on the table so you can almost see your partner—you can almost see each other. But the ropes bind you tight and don't allow you to move a single muscle. Not even your tongue, thanks to the gag. Everything's tight and uncomfortable, but it won't last long. The chef starts carving up the two of you and placing pieces of your meat on plates for each of the diners like selections of sushi.

You don't last through the meal.

You chose poorly.

"I don't think I can," you tell them. "I'm looking for someone."

They children look at each other again. The boy tells the girl, "Hasn't he found someone?"

"Two someone's, I believe," the girl says.

They turn their attention back to you, frowning exaggeratedly.

"It's a guessing game," the boy says.

"Yeah, guessing," the girl says. "Guess what we've found."

You shake your head, but you feel compelled to respond anyhow. "Won't you give me a clue?"

"That's not playing fair," the girl says.

"Oh, we can give you a clue," the boy says. "But it'll cost you."

The girl looks at the boy. The boy looks back and smiles until she returns it, then they're looking at you again.

"Blood," they say, simultaneously.

They leap at you simultaneously. They're small, but fast, and impossibly strong. Their nails are like razors. They slash at you, cutting deeply, burying their teeth in your legs and back. You drop backwards, trying to reach a weapon of some sort—one of those chisels, perhaps—but they drag you to the marble floor. Once they've got you down, there's no getting up again—until someone else steps into the room and says, "Children."

They leap immediately off you, holding their hands behind their backs in some gesture of innocence, though the girl takes a moment to wipe your blood from her mouth. They look at the newcomer, a man who might be their father, whose eyes are so blue they glow.

Find a weapon. Go to Page 259.

Wait and see what happens. Go to Page 359.

You tell her you're merely interested in old cathedrals, that you'd never known this one existed, that you're fascinated in all things old and sacred.

She smiles at this, though maybe she doesn't believe you. "I am old," she says, though she doesn't look it. "I am sacred. Would you worship me?" Her smiles grows, her incisors are sharp like a canine's, and you wonder briefly if her lips are so red because of lipstick or blood.

Don't. Go to Page 161.

Worship her. Go to Page 340.

You accept the wine. The man has his own glass. He raises it, says, "*Salut*," and takes a good mouthful.

You do the same.

The poison works fast. Because the wine isn't wine, it's the fungus, the same liquid version in the corpse's glass, and it's replacing the blood in your veins. You try to move, but the weight of the fungus, the weight of everything, slows your steps, and forces you to sit. Only for a moment, you tell yourself. Until you catch your breath.

The fungus, however, is already drawing you down into the ground, and you'll never rise again. The ghost of the man in the wine cellar kneels next to you and says, "That's exactly how it happened to me."

You chose poorly.

Walking on the rain-slick stone roof is impossible, so you crawl on hands and knees, making your way up the slope toward a giant brass bell. There's nothing to hold, and the rooftop is slick, but you manage not to slide off the edge before reaching the bell tower.

You climb in.

It's not dry here. The wind whips the rain around in every direction. The storm is getting worse.

There's a single wood door. It takes effort to open. The door resists as you pull, but eventually surrenders and allows you entry. The stairs wind tightly and descend into darkness. You pull the door shut behind you—hiding your tracks maybe?—and plunge into utter, total darkness.

Something crawls over your foot.

You pause, briefly, unable to hear anything over the storm. Another rat—it's definitely a rat, you can feel its tail—runs across your foot. Another takes a bite of your ankle.

The suddenness of it startles you, and that's all it takes to lose your footing on the uneven stone steps. In the next moment, you're tumbling down the stairs, down and around for who knows how long before you manage to stop yourself. You hear your wrist snap right at the end. The pain is excruciating.

You try to catch your breath. You're scraped and probably bruised, you may have fractured a rib, your wrist is definitely useless and probably swelling, and now your eyesight is playing tricks on you because you're sure there's a dark smoke drifting through the darkness around you, when in fact you can't see anything.

Another rat bites your thigh before you get up.

After that, it's a swarm—a plague of rats, actually, hungry for your blood, hungry for the soft flesh between your fingers and on your ears. When you try to rise, a hand presses your chest down and prevents it. "Shush," she says—whoever she is—"The children are starved."

The *children*—the rats—feed on you until they're sated.

You chose poorly.

John Urbancik

Fortune favors the bold. You crawl into the smooth, cold crypt, and release the lever. You hear the mechanism of the door, like a giant clock, operating behind you; then the marble door is scraping open against the stone floor.

You climb out of the crypt backwards. The shadows seem to have shifted, perhaps because the open door now blocks part of the light in this corner of the crypt. The door reveals a narrow passage to an inner sanctum behind the tombs.

You squeeze through and find a room with a comfortable reading chair, a lamp, a table, and a selection of religious texts—not exclusively Christian—you see Islamic and Buddhist symbology, and lettering you can't decipher.

Seated at the chair—seriously, you didn't see her when you entered the room, though she's obviously there now—is an elderly woman with a thick leather-bound book open in her hands. She looks at you with ancient eyes. "Why must you disturb me?"

Lie to her. Go to Page 310.

Tell her the truth. Go to Page 312.

Leave without a word. Go to Page 369.

You go back.

If the man in the church told the truth, you would've found someone, but there was no one here and there seems to be no place else to search. You trace your steps back through the catacombs and then the racks of wine, you climb the stairs, and you return to the ground level of the cathedral. The man continues to kneel there, though he glances in your direction.

You can check out the alcoves and doors. Go to Page 266.

Or you can leave the cathedral. Go to Page 343.

You hesitate. You reach for the knob, but you don't open it. With so many eyes on you, you're convinced it's some sort of trick, a trap, a game you can't understand.

You step away from the door.

You say, "No. I can't do that."

The woman, the vampire queen, shakes her head and steps away. "Then run."

All around, the shadows move. There's two directions to run: toward the cathedral's exit, or deeper into the cathedral.

To run for the exit, go to Page 299.

To go through the door anyhow, go to Page 345.

To run into the cathedral, go to Page 368.

You have no plan. You simply can't allow what's about to happen. You rush forward, grabbing a sharp knife from the table. You don't go for the chef or the old man or any of the diners, but start working at the ropes binding your partner.

The old man touches your shoulder and says, "It's too late for that."

You turn and stab him with the knife, plunge it right into his chest without thinking. He looks down at the weapon, then into your eyes, and smiles. "Ah, but that's not the way to do it." He withdraws the knife from his chest, wipes it with a white napkin—there's surprisingly little blood—then buries it in your shoulder.

Through your shoulder, he hits a major artery, then twists the knife.

"That," he says through the agonizing pain, "is how you do it." Your blood sprays his pale face. The other diners are anxious to get closer, to take their share of your blood.

They drink you dry, then lay you next to your partner and dine on the meat of both of you.

You chose poorly.

"Children," the man says again, not even acknowledging you, "what have we told you about playing with your food?"

You've heard enough. You go for weapons anyway, but you don't have a chance to reach them. He's got you by the back of your neck. He lifts you off your feet.

"Enjoy this one, children," he says. "We've got the other to sate us."

The other must be your partner, your lover, lost somewhere else in this cathedral. You'll never know, though. He pieces the back of your neck with a fingernail like a needle, slips its between vertebrae and cuts your spine.

He drops you. You fall, unable to move arms or legs. You feel pain—that's not fair—you feel everything, but can move nothing below your neck. You work your jaw, you complain bitterly, you even scream. The children tear sloppily into you. You're completely unable to resist.

It's a messy, painful, even arduous death, and it lasts longer than it should, but it's final.

You chose poorly.

"That would be great," you say.

"You shan't be my only guest this night," the stranger tells you. He leads you along the edge of the roof, steadying you with a hand that hardly seems to make any effort, until you reach the tower itself. "Please, make your way through the cloisters to the vestry, where we shall dine."

As you step under the dome of the bell tower and out of the rain, the stranger has disappeared entirely.

From here, there's only one direction to go: down the dark, narrow stairs.

They wind tightly. The steps are uneven and your shoes are slick, so you hold the stone walls on both sides to prevent an inconvenient slide and tumble.

Down, you descend, dozens of steps then hundreds of steps then thousands. It seems the stairs from the tower never end.

After what feels like forever, finally they end at a thick wood door. You have to put your shoulder to it to force it open.

On the other side, you discover a crypt.

Fires in sconces light the crypt, which contains the final remains of a dozen or more priests, bishops, and saints. Several blocks of marble have names engraved on them, but many are empty and one is open.

The open tomb is empty.

The ceiling is high here, but not as high as inside the cathedral. The lights are dim and the shadows thick, and someone — or something — breathes in the darkness.

It's your partner.

You run to embrace. Too late, you see your lover's incisors have changed, sharpened and lengthened, and they're buried in your neck before you can react.

"Excellent," the stranger says from behind you, guiding the two of you toward the open tomb. Your partner drags you in. You — you try to resist, but you're not that strong, and you've already lost blood.

The stranger closes the crypt behind you, locking you and your lover in eternal darkness. It's almost romantic, except for the pain of teeth and the reek of sour breath and the dizziness that eventually overtakes you.

Your lover consumes you in the tomb. Perhaps sometime after, the stranger releases your partner, now a vampire. Perhaps not.

You chose poorly.

You descend again into the wine cellar. But the pristine barrels have been coated by dust and grime and, seemingly, decades of neglect. The man is gone. Several barrels have been smashed open with an axe or hatchet of some sort.

Around the corner, the racks of wine bottles are empty except for spider webs and rats and shifting shadows thick as honey.

There, sitting in the center of the room, is the man you'd spoken with, the husk of the man, shallowed out, gutted and empty. His skin is pale and his eyes are milky and some sort of black fungus has overtaken the lower half of his body.

The corpse stares blankly, but for a moment—maybe it's a trick of the light—it seems to focus on you. He clutches a wine glass in his dead hand. Inside, there's a black liquid more like the fungus than any wine you've ever seen. The odor is earthy, thick and pungent. Involuntarily, you step back—to find there's no longer a room with wine barrels but a solid brick wall, the bricks crumbling and decrepit like all the bricks of this version of the wine cellar.

A ghost of the man—a shimmering, half real, half translucent version of the corpse seated against a column in the middle of the wine cellar—says, "It's an excellent year." He's offering a freshly poured glass of something. The wine looks positively real.

Accept the wine. Go to Page 353.

Leave, and don't accept the wine. Go to Page 363.

"Thank you, no," you say, refusing the wine.

The man smiles. He says, "That's what I should have said."
As you pass him and his corpse, the ghost of him drinks the wine
you'd refused.

*Back at the entrance to the cellar, you can follow the
softest possible strains of tinny music. Go to Page 65.*

*You can go the other way, toward utter silence. Go to
Page 83.*

Or you can leave the cellar. Go to Page 289.

These stairs go straight down for a fairly long way, until the stone walls give way to rock, and you find yourself in a cave of some sort. First, there are rows of wine bottles, like in a wine cellar, but these quickly lead to rows of bones. Femurs first, then ribs, and the archways carved into the cave are lined with skulls.

The catacombs go on for a ways, turning at seemingly random intervals, the bones arranged in groupings—fingers here, hips there. The electric lights give way to gas sconces, but there's still light, at least for a little while.

The catacombs end abruptly at a wall, and there seems to be no place left to go.

To look for some sort of hidden door, go to Page 272.

To go back, go to Page 356.

You ignore the house and walk to the cemetery. It's attached to the cathedral, not the house, though the two must be connected. Again, there may be more questions here than you care to discover corresponding answers.

The church is a rectangular plot of land with a gate. Standing at the gate, looking over the stones, all those crosses and cherubs and weeping angels, you see no indication of your partner or anyone else.

It's not too late to go back to the house. You can walk up to the front door and announce yourself. Go to Page 2.

You can sneak around the back and climb in through a window. Go to Page 3.

You can enter through the cellar doors in the back. Go to Page 4.

Or you can pass through the gate into the cemetery. Go to Page 329.

The second door you try opens and leads, through a transept of thick woods, solid marble, and vibrant paintings, into the sacristy. There's a large wooden table covered with ornate carvings and a variety of jewels with flat file drawers beneath it. Opening one reveals blueprints to the cathedral in a series of sheer, nearly transparent sheets of paper the size of posters. Mostly faded, they reveal only a few words in another language.

A series of six paintings on either side of the sacristy portray each of the apostles, with Jesus himself at the center, alone on the far wall. One of paintings has a fresh red X through it, and a question scrawled underneath: *Where Judas?*

The domed ceiling is broken into panels and painted as a night sky, cloudless, full of stars, planets out of proportion, nebulae, and a vibrant line down the middle representing the Milky Way.

The walls are a series of cabinets and drawers, presumably housing religious vestments, ceremonial clothes for the priests, and records of the church, but you open a few to make sure your partner isn't hiding—or hidden—in one of them.

An arch leads to another room. To enter, go to Page 337.

To explore the sacristy more thoroughly, go to Page 344.

John Urbancik

You struggle, though it seems hopeless. After twenty seconds of it, the stranger says, "I shan't catch you."

Then he lets go.

Briefly, you're righting yourself, backing away from the man who might be a vampire of the most obvious type. You face him even as you back away, but the stones are slick and the slope is steep. You slip, and go over the edge, and though you flail your arms as you fall, you cannot fly.

You crash to the ground. Bones shatter, blood splatters, but the pain is brief because death is quick.

You chose poorly.

You know you can't make the front door. There are too many of them. So you do the one thing you think they won't expect. You run into the shadows of the cathedral.

The shadows swallow you.

The shadows envelop you.

The shadows crush you.

You chose poorly.

Maybe you nod, or smile, or something—but what you definitely do is retreat down the passage. But when you reach the marble door, it's been closed. You never heard it move a second time.

There's barely room to turn around, and the old woman is at the other edge of the passage, preventing you from going forward. She's shaking her head. "The modern world," she says, "is so rude."

She seems too big to get through the passage, but she enters. She smiles, and her teeth are too big for her mouth. There's no retreat, and no room to fight, but you do the best you can as she grabs at you with clawed fingers and, unaffected by your feeble attempts to defend yourself, ravages your body, shredding skin and gulping blood, sighing and moaning as she does so, practically hyperventilating, as though she doesn't often get a chance to feed like this.

You chose poorly.

ACKNOWLEDGMENTS

I wrote most of this book in Spain
with the support of Mery-et Lescher.

I employed a number of First Readers,
inviting them to play a game.
Thanks also to the Five Horsemen,
my various inspirations,
anyone who has ever taught me anything,
the ghost of Edgar Allan Poe,
and all my Pulp Heroes,
and the many, many books I read in the 80s.

Rebecca Narron helped by providing
some of the stock photos used on the cover.
Some of the photos are mine,
including Scarlett Del Sol,
and the cemetery.

Thanks Mom.

I always miss people.
But you are all in my heart.
Or running away with it
still pumping in your hands.

As always: thanks to
Sabine and the Rose Fairy.

ABOUT THE AUTHOR

John Urbancik may have found himself, once or twice, in a horror story, and either he's lived to tell the tale or his ghost types 125 words a minute.

His first novel, *Sins of Blood and Stone*, came out in 2002, and he has never figured out how to stop. His books include collections of poetry and photography, a nonfiction book based on the 100 episode run of his podcast *Inkstains* (based on his three year-long projects of the same name), the *DarkWalker* series, *Stale Reality* (also available in Russian), and *Once Upon a Time in Midnight*.

Born on a small island in the northeast United States called Manhattan, he is currently sequestered in an undisclosed location in the woods of Pennsylvania near the Susquehanna River.

www.DarkFluidity.com

ALSO BY JOHN URBANCIK

NOVELS
Sins of Blood and Stone
Breath of the Moon
Once Upon a Time in Midnight
Stale Reality
The Corpse and the Girl from Miami
DarkWalker 1: Hunting Grounds
DarkWalker 2: Inferno
DarkWalker 3: The Deep City
DarkWalker 4: Armageddon
DarkWalker 5: Ghost Stories
DarkWalker 6: Other Realms

NOVELLAS
A Game of Colors
The Rise and Fall of Babylon (with Brian Keene)
Wings of the Butterfly
House of Shadow and Ash
Necropolis
Quicksilver
Beneath Midnight
Zombies vs. Aliens vs. Robots vs. Cowboys vs.
Ninja vs. Investment Bankers vs. Green Berets
Colette and the Tiger
Clockwork Ravens
The Night Carnival

COLLECTIONS
Shadows, Legends & Secrets
Sound and Vision
Tales of the Fantastic and the Phantasmagoric

POETRY
John the Revelator
Odyssey

NONFICTION
InkStained: On Creativity, Writing, and Art

INKSTAINS
Multiple volumes

Made in the USA
Middletown, DE
04 March 2023